A Pernicious Gene

By

Elle Fran Williams

Introduction

First of all, let me say I am merely the story teller, the mouthpiece if you like. My name is Edwina Tennyson, known to my friends as Eddie, and to my colleagues and more brainy and educated clients as The Poet, for obvious reasons (or behind my back, I think, as Po)! I am a specialist in psychiatric medicine, and, since I am also a workaholic and perhaps even more relevantly, an insomniac, I also have a first class Law degree, though I have never actually practised at the bar. Over the past three decades I have been working predominantly with damaged and - to my mind anyway - fascinating personalities, including psychopaths and sociopaths, who are brought before the courts for major crimes.

I am now retired, but was part of a team employed to advise the Courts on questions of competence or fitness to stand trial - to sort out the merely scheming from the genuinely afflicted - the wheat from the chaff, if you like. It was much rarer for my work to be with younger people - it was usually sad, bad or mad adults - as it happens mostly men, though that, I believe was purely an accident of circumstance. My expertise was considered more with 'grown ups', but that was the dilemma. Helen Collier was, technically, a grown up. Her crime had certainly not lacked a deliberation and a plan, but had it also demonstrated naivety and an inability to see the true consequences and finality of such a course of action?

Sometimes I was brought in to decide whether somebody was 'fit to plead', that is whether they were so mentally unsound that they were in no position to know what they had done, whether they had done it, or that what they had done was criminal. Other times I was called in after the trial proper, when the verdict had gone against the accused, because the judge needed to have some kind of professional guidance on the capacity of a person before deciding on an appropriate sentence. The latter was particularly helpful where the person on trial had pleaded guilty. With a shorter trial, with no real argument put up by the defendant, and sometimes the defendant not even giving evidence on their own behalf, there was much less time for them to be heard and 'judged'. A longer trial - an argued trial - allowed the sentence, within the law, to be influenced by proper evidence, as well as the person's remorse, demeanour, or just sheer 'likeability'.

So in 33 years, I have only worked with 12 adolescents - that is young persons who were not quite adults, but not quite children either. Such cases stay long in one's memory, but even amongst those, my most disturbing, without a shadow of a doubt, was Helen Collier.

This was Helen's story - the background to her crime - an awful and irreversible crime - but one that was perhaps inevitable.

PART ONE

Chapter 1:   Meet the Colliers

They just did not like her!   It was an individual view, but it was also a collective one.   None of them could have told you - or more especially told her - why.   It was just a fact.   It was not her so much as what she represented.

She had arrived out of the blue one day hand in hand with the only remaining 'man' of the house: their son, brother, uncle, James. He was a tyrant, but he was their tyrant!

Here he was all 6ft 1 inches of him, smiling, fawning, simpering over this 5ft 1-inch OLD woman.   In truth, she was not an 'old woman', but she was considerably older than him - nine years older in fact: he was 25, she was 34.   She was not unattractive, certainly not unpleasant, to look at, but neither was she anything to write home about.

James (Jimmy) had been one of seven children, five girls, two boys. Two of the girls had died in their early years from diphtheria, which together with scarlet fever was the fate of many babies and young children at that time.   To add to their woes, Charlie, the second eldest of the children, and one of the only two boys, had picked a fight with the wrong individual outside a dance hall when he was nineteen, and had been knifed to death. The fact that the murderer was serving 18 years for the offence was of no comfort or consolation to the family. The Judge, when summing up at the trial, had expressed the opinion - surprisingly outspokenly, indeed vehemently - that Charlie had himself gone out looking for trouble, and had instigated the fight. He had not quite gone so far as to say that he got what he deserved, but he most definitely left everybody in the courtroom under no illusion that the facts bore that judgement out. He could not escape from the fact that the offender, Stephen Ryan, should not have been carrying a blade with him in any case, so it had been impossible for the verdict to be anything other than manslaughter. But that obviously saved Stephen Ryan from the gallows and started a whole new wave of resentment and bile within Charlie's family. The judge's name was Maurice Sachs. The names of both of these principal characters in the tragedy were significant, since the family had already decidedly racist and xenophobic tendencies - nay, say it as it was, they were unanimously bigots of the first order and fed off of one another's prejudice and ignorance.

Don't get me wrong. Don't for a minute believe that these people had no friends; that they were shunning of the world and shunned by the world. Far from it!

Writing this, many years down the line, I have seen history - personal and global history - through more dispassionate eyes. Those were different times!   Life was different then!
In the years immediately before the Second World War, life was ordered, straightforward, even for many, quite pleasant.   There were hierarchies, but expectations were modest, so disappointments were less debilitating.   Apart from a few 'Commies' - agitators, who were largely either ignored, despised or ridiculed -   the masses, by and large, did not really moan about their lot in life. People had their place, and knew their place: in their home; in their community; in society as a whole.

Communities were more like communes.   Neighbours were often related, and, even if not, were definitely more involved in one another's lives, loves, and tragedies. Generations of families lived close, often in the same house, if not, then in the same street, or within a stone's throw of one another.   Mostly people did not stray far from what they were, what they knew and who they knew.

Cars were not within the means of most 'ordinary' people, there was no television to keep people locked behind closed doors. 'Entertainment' was the radio, the public house, the local cinema and sometimes in some places the Music Hall. But people were generally helpful to one another; front doors had locks but frequently no keys. Children played in the street from dawn to dusk, only returning to eat, and fear was more to do with the knock on the door from the rent man or tally man than about a lost child, or even a tragic road traffic accident.

That did not mean that behind closed doors peace and harmony reigned supreme. It was not only in mainland Europe that the evil face of racism and bigotry was to be found. That was the era of '*no Blacks, no Irish, no dogs*' in the windows. Under the surface, there was a mistrust of the different, the exotic.

That having been said, in past times, most communities usually welcomed 'visitors'. Those passing through or those with something to trade. People offered hospitality and friendship, in the short term when advantages were shared and generosity not abused. But hordes of those 'visitors' moving in and imposing themselves and their way of life on the tribe was a different kettle of fish! People feared just what they may take from them. More important than their possessions - their houses, their jobs, their loved ones, their security - they feared that they would water down their very selves, their very identity. So put into context, the 'family', the Collier family, was not unique, not even conventionally 'wicked'. To the world they were funny, outgoing, welcoming, even attractive, people who smiled in the right places, were the life and soul of any party, and left a rosy glow on first acquaintance with all, or at least most, people. The trouble was that they were all chameleons. Behind closed doors they were caustic, condemning, belittling and found anybody 'foreign', 'different' or even 'uppity' an endless source of amusement and castigation. They fed off one another's bile and prejudice and unfortunately, because with it they also possessed comedic and mimicking skills, to those who were of a similar ilk, they made very entertaining company. A deadly and contaminating combination.

Though the family was extensive and close knit, for the purposes of this story, there are really only four main protagonists, so please forgive my reluctance to name and describe them all. Suffice it to say, that the description of all, or at least most, of them would be similar, only differing in age, stature and hair colouring. By nature, and thinking, with a few exceptions who needed either to be strong willed themselves, or keep their mouths well and truly shut, they were decidedly cloned.

Margaret Helen, (Maggie) (61) was the matriarch (obviously referred to as Mum, Gran, or Genghis) - depending upon the relationship to the person addressing her and sometimes her mood. Frequently as 'Aggie-Maggie' by her various grandchildren if they were being cheeky and spoiled, which was frequently the case. Maggie had few boundaries as far as her grandchildren were concerned, and however bold or perverse they got for their own parents, they were always protected from retribution by her, since only she was allowed to chastise them - which she almost never did!

Maggie was tall and extremely slim - indeed one could say thin, almost unhealthily so. There was not an extra ounce of flesh upon her body, not because she stinted herself, or anybody else for that matter, of food - good hearty food, nothing fancy, but definitely designed to sustain her kith and kin through their busy days, and far beyond. Maggie's physique was down to her almost permanent state of nervous energy and 'need' to be doing something. She seemed to find it impossible to sit still for any length of time, apart from one 'fetish'! Maggie had long, lustrous hair, which, despite having gone prematurely silver white, during her forties, was her pride and joy. She would beaver about her home, or the neighbourhood all day - and sometimes much of the night, but as soon as any - and each sometimes - of her grandchildren walked through the door, out would come the brush, she would pull out one of the upright wooden kitchen chairs, and she would sit quietly while they brushed her hair until it shone - again and again. It was a ritual - perhaps just a way of sharing some still time with her grandchildren, or perhaps she just liked her hair brushed - who can tell. But listening to Gladys the children - more particularly as they became older - were resigned rather than appreciative of this 'close time' and often used to try to plan their arrivals home to give them the best chance of avoiding the 'chore'. Apart from that, they loved their grandmother who gave them treats, encouraged their company - sometimes even if that meant them missing school! It was not unheard of for Maggie to take one of them off to the cinema on a school day, together with a bag of homemade biscuits or cakes, denying all knowledge and responsibility if - and sometimes when - the truancy was noticed and their mothers complained. Somehow the children seemed to know it was their role in the escapade to 'keep their trap shut' and take the blame. They would be rewarded in due course!

Eleanor (Lena) was 46, her oldest daughter, born when Maggie was not yet 16, and long before Maggie's ultimate marriage, which came relatively late in life, but still like the rest, according to her, fathered by William George. *(Having researched the family subsequently, I think this is possibly a slightly tongue in cheek claim on her part, but .... Anyway, as a story closely following the female side of the family, William George is of little consequence, but we will return to him a bit later on).* On the face of it, Lena did not appear to have any children, though, from my subsequent conversations with her sister, Gladys, I personally believe that two things were possible: she had given birth to children, but these had not survived, and/or she had given birth to children, but one or more of these had been passed off as the children of her mother, Maggie. The reasons for my surmising this will become clearer later on. Lena was only about 5ft 4in tall, and unlike her mother she was well-covered and rotund. She seemed quite solid, though, and it was more a question of being sturdy - stocky, rather than carrying too much fat. That being said, she was by far the least 'active' of the women and compared to the rest she was slow and cumbersome. That, though, was compared to the others who were almost hyperactive; permanently moving and frequently in a stew about something or other.

Gladys Josephine (Glad) was the second daughter, some 8 years younger than Lena, and the mother of **Beatrice (Beattie)**, now aged 17, still living with her grandmother but officially 'courting' and hoping to marry when accommodation close to the family could be located, hopefully in time for the arrival of her baby, which had a due date some five months hence.

Gladys was wiry like her mother, but dark, almost Mediterranean in appearance. Had one been cruel one might have described her as 'swarthy'. I assumed, when I met her, and met her mother briefly, that perhaps Maggie's hair had been very dark - black perhaps - when she was younger. Frequently, I think, people with black hair tend to go grey - even completely silver - very early, so Gladys did seem to take after her mother the most of all of the women, in appearance, but also, perhaps, in temperament and outlook. (This was borne out in subsequent times when Gladys was the last one remaining at home, and became the confidante of her mother, and was handed the mantle of protecting the family. I believe this was not only because the others had drifted away, but that they had drifted away, because the bond was stronger between Gladys and Maggie, than between the rest. I think she was the most trusted of them all, because Maggie saw much of herself in Gladys.)

(N.B. Many years after the tragedy of Helen, Gladys surprisingly became my most honest and most instructive source of information after the event. Though, on the face of it, she should have been the last person on the planet to empathise with or apologise for Helen, nonetheless that was how it was.)

Beatrice was tall, like her grandmother and mother, but her hair was mousy (at least at the roots!) though most of the time the colour came out of a bottle. She was blonde by choice rather than by nature. Other than that, she was 'ordinary', neither plain nor beautiful. She was young for her years, despite her pregnancy, and tended to be petulant and demanding of attention. *(N.B. These observations are all 'after the fact' and from photographs, descriptions and talking to her mother and to Helen, since I never actually met her during her lifetime. I also had some conversations with my erstwhile colleagues who had known her during her years of incarceration).*

Constance Margaret (Connie) was Maggie's youngest surviving daughter. She was now 29 and had two children, Cecilia (Cissie) and Ronald (Ronnie) aged 6 and 4 who also lived with their grandmother.

In addition, Freddie (7) and Georgie (5), Gladys's other children, Beattie's siblings, also lived with their grandmother. Gladys had also 'lost' two babies at birth and had several miscarriages over the years. She did seem to love her children, and had apparently not given them up as much as merely complied with the 'law according to Maggie', very much the matriarch of the family, and whose word was paramount. There were also two other children - adolescents - who sometimes lived with Maggie and sometimes lived wherever 'home' was, but who were more elusive and difficult to assign: Harry, who was about 17 and Eddie who was 15 or so. Suffice it to say, the house was never silent, and always a mass of activities and bodies. *(On more than one occasion, unfortunately, that was a statement only too close to the mark - a statement of fact rather than merely an unfortunate form of words! One such occasion was assumed to be the root cause and catalyst for Helen's subsequent actions and another the reason for her current incarceration.)*

So into this family, Jimmy brought his new girlfriend - woman friend really, they supposed, since she was hardly a girl. Jimmy, to them, as the only male of significance left in the family, was special.

The official patriarch, William George (Bill), their father, had long since given up any attempt at being the man of the house. He had tried dominance, even physical violence, for the first few years, but had gradually capitulated. He had given in without too much fight in recent years, having been systematically worn down by the surrounding females of the species, who now fed him, watered him, but largely ignored him. He was pleased to not have to do battle, and had happily retreated into his armchair and his pretence of senility and deafness.

It is necessary, in order to relate the facts as accurately as possible, to acknowledge that there were other 'men' holding peripheral roles in this almost exclusively feminine ménage. Three of the women had homes elsewhere; all of them had husbands; all of them had lives outside the environs of number 7 Percival Street, the two storey (and a basement) abode of the current matriarch and her unfortunately now toothless (both physically and metaphorically!) spouse.

The marriages were merely a convention. The husbands, none of whom were by nature wimps or cowards, had nonetheless given up on any expectations that they might have had of a 'normal' household, where their wives cooked, cleaned, obeyed and presented themselves, clean, aired and ready to perform their conjugal responsibilities in good order when the time was right. In most houses, in 'those days', husbands were expected to be masters within their own households. I would malign those husbands if I implied that they were too cowed or wimpish to object or make a stand, but they had certainly got worn down and in anything but outward appearances, the relationships were a sham. Divorce was certainly not the norm and indeed none of them, I am sure, considered there would be anything gained. The women were just not the sort to accept that the rules within such 'marriages' applied to them.

They all just created their own rules. Though still ostensibly living under the same roof, and bringing home a pay packet now and again, the men had all decided that their allegiance lay in a different direction, mostly the nearest public house, or 'bookie'. They were maligned and verbally abused constantly by the women for their drunken and feckless ways, but in truth even had they been the epitome of morality, dependency and piety it still would not have saved them from the witty, scathing and mischievous tongues of their womenfolk. So the men found other ways of escaping their disillusionment… until they got 'called up' and joined the armed forces to fight for king and country, which unfortunately also had the prospect of a more permanent and decidedly less healthy change of circumstances.

So the men, with the exception of Jimmy, were of absolutely no significance. Jimmy - who was one of their own, not just an outsider who had been allowed to join the family in order to comply with convention and to ensure its continuance - had been allowed to take on the mantle of 'Tarzan' to all of the 'Janes'. He had ruled quite successfully since reaching maturity, barking out his orders, sometimes even emphasising these with palpable aggression, strong language and even, if his mood was bad, the back of his hand. With his mother's acquiescence, even pride, he demanded his rightful place in the household, insisting, whilst the various sisters and nieces were young adults, and before they had homes, husbands, children of their own, that they earn their keep, pull their weight and generally toe the line. Jimmy had never been vocal with his opinions, and left the character assassinations and mimicry to others. On the other hand, he had never shown any indication that he felt any different and certainly never tried to change their views. They all assumed that he agreed, but that their skylarking and hilarity - not infrequently also vulgarity - were beneath his dignity - just women talk.

The new woman in James's life then was Elizabeth Mary Quinlan. She was only an inch over 5ft tall, and tiny in stature, but definitely not in personality. She was quick with the come-back and permanently upbeat, with an answer for everything, and a 'way about her' which made her not just good company, but welcome company. She was intelligent and most certainly nobody's fool. She had lived around the best - perhaps not born to the best - but she most definitely knew what the best was and saw herself as aspiring for better. Anybody that met her had no difficulty in believing that she would achieve better too.

It is no wonder then that the hen house was rattled by the sudden introduction of this new woman in Jimmy's life. Worse still, over the ensuing months, it became quite clear that this pocket rocket had their love-struck brother right under her thumb. He was acquiescent - even participating in his own emasculation - and in time, horror upon horror, he asked his beloved to marry him.

To their shock and discomfiture, his betrothed was Irish, Roman Catholic, fearless, intelligent, certainly as loquacious and vocal as them: she could out talk them, out act them, out story tell them, she called their bluff at every turn, and she saw right through them, entering into their territory and going eyeball to eyeball with them without even blinking. They were alarmed. They knew she felt their hostility. They might show politeness, even consideration, outwardly - not least because they were all sure that, despite all, Jimmy would take 'her' side. They did not blame him for this - she, the Irish shrew, had him brainwashed, but he had a temper, and until they could 'turn him back' they were not brave enough to outwardly take on his 'Elizabeth'. They were even offended that she insisted on being called Elizabeth, not Lizzie, or Betty, or even

Beth (though that would be a bit 'snobby'!). She even insisted on calling Jimmy, James! She was looking down on them, since all of them had pet names. She thought she was superior.

From Elizabeth's perspective, she knew their capabilities, she had their measure. Suffice it to say, she had supreme faith in her own abilities, her own determination. At no point did she believe that they could oust her from James's affection, or deflect them from their plans. In a bright world of love and plans, and hopes and dreams James was oblivious to all of this. Had he been more attached to the earthly plain, he of all people should have realised that Elizabeth had no way of knowing that it was dangerous to underestimate the sheer strength and determination of the 'clan'. He would have been able to warn her that she should not discount the speed with which they were capable of moving from verbal to physical assault. To them she was a non-person; an inferior being, a beetle under their heel. They were a superior class of being. There were no 'woodlice in their woodpile'. The family had been insular and isolationist for years. The unfortunate circumstances of Charlie's death had only given them a point of focus, an excuse, a justification for their views. An Irishman had taken their beloved Charlie. A 'Jew boy' had called him a thug and a bully. He had all but said he deserved what he got! There was no way that some

Irish old hag was going to take Jimmy too. He needed to be saved from himself - from dishonouring his family, his race, his culture, his …… his creed!

At the time of their meeting, which was 1937, there was no way of knowing that within a couple of years, the world would be turned into chaos and calamity. Elizabeth had been working as a housekeeper in a grand house in Golders Green in North London for the past four years. She had been in England since she was 16, having left her native Ireland just before the 1916 rebellion which saw the streets and by-ways of that benighted land run red with the blood of both the Irish Republican Army and the British soldiers sent to quell the fighting and protect British interests. *(It was not helpful either that within the family, one of the men, Archie - Lena's - I guess nowadays he would be a 'partner' - was an ex professional soldier. Archie had replaced Lena's legitimate husband some several years before when she had, not unreasonably, got fed up of constant black eyes and fat lips. Archie had been a 'Black and Tan', one of the British soldiers sent to Ireland to quell the insurrection. Having fought in that bloody conflict, he had naturally brought back his own stories (some justified and truthful, some biased and manufactured) of the bastards and vermin that populated that horrible backward and ungodly land.)*

After arriving in England, as can be imagined under the circumstances, Elizabeth had suffered a few difficult years at first. She was very young and she was in a land which was in the throes of a very bloody conflict with her own. With hardship had come resilience and more importantly guile and canniness. Though she was from a very large family - indeed a family originally of 13 - but only six were surviving by the time Elizabeth left home - they had all been very well educated and more importantly had the gift of the gab and an ability to assume whatever personality served them best at any given time. All of the family would have made Oscar winning actors, had that ever been a career path that occurred to any of them. It was useful and a comfort also that two of her sisters were also working in England, one much older than Elizabeth having come some years before, and one a year or two after her. They had all started lowly 'in service' but all had gradually got their feet under the table and two were now in good households, one as a cook, the other a housekeeper. The third sister escaped from 'service' when her then far-sighted employer saw how gifted she was with a needle and thread and decided that she could use her talents, when a 'backer' was persuaded to front a fashion house in the heart of London. None of the sisters had up to that time married. Elizabeth was the first.

By 1938, Elizabeth was well and truly settled. She was personable, intelligent, shrewd and adaptable. Knowing what to say, and when to say it. She thought a lot, but knew when to hold her tongue and when to stand her ground. Though she was tiny, both in height and stature, she made up for this in presence and charisma. Her then employers, a successful Jewish family, who had originally come to England from Europe some thirty years before, were becoming, by this time, somewhat concerned with the situation that was threatening to engulf their relatives still living in Germany, Holland and Poland. Elizabeth understood the plight and the worries which beset the family, having endured similar worries and anxieties during her early years in England when war was raging in her own homeland and two more of her brothers had been lost to them.

The Greenbergs were sad that they might lose Elizabeth to marriage, but were nonetheless very kind and accommodating of her relationship with James. To the relief of all, it was agreed, Elizabeth being something of a free spirit and not following the norm which was for wives to stop work when they married, that she would remain working, obviously no longer resident, but coming daily to continue her duties as before. James was comfortable with this, or professed himself to be so, though it was probable in reality that he had little say in the matter!

Within James's insular family the marriage ceremony itself was an even bigger source of disharmony. Not only did Elizabeth insist on getting married in a Roman Catholic church, but somehow 'coerced' their poor Jimmy into converting too. Worse, he did not just seem to have 'gone along with this', but seemed to actually take the whole charade seriously. He went to Mass regularly, he seemed to take issue nowadays with their language, their conversation, their …. their everything! True, he had not been too involved in their chit chat before, but neither had he showed any disapproval or disagreement. No, it was her. She had turned his head, and she had turned him into this ….' this puppet, this effing arse licker, this bloody lapdog!'

So after the wedding, no honeymoon, no real 'do', though a few close friends were invited for a celebratory drink. Neither of Elizabeth's sisters were able to attend, so the only real guests on her side were two Irish friends and their children. The children got on famously with the younger Colliers and the adult 'diddycoys' as Maggie was prone to call them (indeed anybody Irish was from the Travellers' race apparently!) were treated politely, and equally politely accepted the begrudged hospitality, more as a requirement than a pleasure.

Elizabeth and James lived in rented accommodation midway between Elizabeth's place of work and 'the family'. *(Though this got bombed during the War whilst James was in the Army so Elizabeth had to move again).* At the time they got married, James worked 'on the dust' (he was a refuse collector with the local council), he started very early, but finished early each day, and normally had Sundays off. Elizabeth usually managed to get Saturdays off since it was the Jewish Sabbath, and the Greenbergs were very much accepting of her need to have some parts of Sunday off, to go to church, and spend some time with James. So weekends, and sometimes parts of other days, as often as possible they went to visit 'the family'. This was never reciprocated, despite James asking several times and several times the family giving assurances that they would come 'soon'. Elizabeth was not sorry about their desire to stay away. She understood their hostility only too well. She only kept the peace because they were James's family and, truthfully, because she was almost enjoying the battle - an unspoken battle, a very one sided battle, but she had the stalwart and almost detached personality to find it all more entertaining than bothersome.

There were some very bitter feelings as war approached, since it was inevitable that discussion included events in Germany, and the plight of the Jewish population. Elizabeth with much more personal experience of war and conflict, and being better informed because of the dire news that was filtering through to the Greenbergs, was, of course, unable to sit and listen to the views of 'the family'. At best this was apathy, at worst it was 'sympathy for' and 'understanding of' Hitler's antipathy towards the 'thieving rogues', the 'scourge of society' - the Jews. Elizabeth was naturally angered by this, and many heated arguments ensued, with deep wounds opened up, and left to fester.

In time, James, in conjunction with the rest of the men, was enlisted into the army and went off to serve his country. It was miraculous how quickly in the family's eyes Hitler suddenly joined the ranks of the ungodly, the most villainous, the most vile man in Christendom!

Maggie was proud as punch that 'her Jimmy' had gone off to sort out that bastard, Hitler, and to win the war. Anybody who had their ear bent by her could be forgiven for thinking he was doing this entirely on his own, by hand to hand combat, like some kind of mediaeval jousting knight! Indeed, at war's end, when Jimmy returned to hearth and home, it was obvious to Maggie that her judgement had been right. Her Jimmy had indeed won the war, and now they were all safe! But a lot was to happen before Jimmy walked once again through his mother's front door.

Chapter 2: Meet Helen Collier, infant, daughter, schoolgirl, murderer

Elizabeth did not find it easy to take to 'the intimate side of married life'. It was definitely more of a duty than a pleasure. To give Jimmy his due he did not broadcast this fact to anybody, least of all his family. This would merely have added to their arsenal of weapons. Elizabeth did, however, appreciate that her duty was to produce a child. She was not sure that she felt like many others of her sex obsessed with the need for a baby, or to be a mother, but convention said that that was the correct order of events: marriage, a baby, another baby, hopefully one of each, then shut up shop…. So her responsibility was clear. But it did not come easy, and despite James's patience and loyalty, Elizabeth did not make the trying all that pleasurable. She was quite prepared to 'lie back and think of England' or perhaps 'Ireland' in her case, but this was obviously quite disheartening for her long-suffering and patient husband. It was probably quite a relief for both when he was called up and left to join his regiment for preliminary training and a soldier's life in the barracks.

Despite those handicaps, and with a grateful nod to a fortnight's leave prior to being sent to fight overseas, absence must have made the heart grow fonder. In early 1942, as bombs were threatening London, Elizabeth gave birth to their first, and as it turned out their only child, a daughter, Helen Elizabeth. The family were inclined to declare a truce as a result of this joyous occasion, and were delighted that the child was called after the matriarch, who was Margaret Helena a. Elizabeth never did let them into the secret that her own mother had also been Helen Elizabeth since what they did not know would not hurt them, and it did no harm for them to go on believing that she had kowtowed to their preferences.

James was informed of his new daughter's birth by letter from a delighted Elizabeth, which eventually reached him, having wended its way across many seas and continents. He was naturally delighted, but also, given the circumstances, somewhat astounded. Despite his surroundings, he was in high spirits and even more anxious now that the war should end, and that he should be able to return home.

Little did he know that by the time he met his daughter, she would be motherless and he would be a widower.

Chapter 3: Murder begets murder!

The final trouble started quite casually. Elizabeth had been diligent in bringing Helen to see her grandmother, aunts and cousins during James's absence. She had also kept in contact with the Greenbergs, though obviously she had had to leave their employ when she fell pregnant. Mrs. Greenberg had given Elizabeth a fur coat that she no longer had enthusiasm for. She had only two sons, both of whom had enlisted and were, much to their parent's concern, fighting in very dangerous parts of the conflict. So since there were, as yet, no daughters-in-law, and Mrs Greenberg was reluctant to tempt providence by just assuming that there would ever be, Elizabeth became the proud owner of the coat, and wasted no time wearing it on a visit to her mother-in-law's.

Two rows erupted that day, fed by jealousy over the coat and its origins, plus, of course, the permanent undercurrent of antagonism which had never really gone away.

It had been the custom within the family for all of the children when they were old enough to live - for reasons that nobody could ever explain, apart from 'it has always been like that' - with their grandmother, in the family home. All of the daughters had complied with this dictat, and as we have already learned several grandchildren were already living there. Up to that day, Elizabeth had never entered into any discussion about this 'custom', knowing that it was just not going to happen to Helen, but preferring to have the argument when it arose, rather than pre-empt it. That day was the day!

Though Helen was little more than 2, the jealousy over the coat made Connie put the question on the table as to when Helen was going to move in and have the company of her cousins. Elizabeth tried very hard to parry the question for as long as she could in order to not have the argument that would end all arguments, but smelling blood, Connie was not going to be deterred and pushed the point. Obviously never was the final reply. Calmly and without getting agitated or intimidated, Elizabeth kept reiterating her decision, and despite the collective hostility around the room, which then began to encompass all of the past grievances, her age, her nationality, her religion, her supposed superiority, her carrying on with that Jew boy who gave her the bloody fur coat, her lack of loyalty to 'poor Jimmy' …… she thought she was Lady Muck, she could clear off back to the Jew boys in Golders Green … and on and on and on.

Elizabeth eventually just smiled. Picked up the fur coat from the back of the chair, narrowing her eyes as she threaded her arms through the sleeves, and said "Well, at last, your true colours are on display. James will never leave his daughter, so you had better get used to the fact that apart from poor old William in the next room, who has to pretend to be senile in order to protect himself from you, you are now what you always wanted to be a coven of witches - not a man amongst you, and now no James either. I wish you all well to wear it! "

As she stooped to pick up Helen who was with two of the other children chewing on dog biscuits under the table, Beattie, who was normally the quietest of the group, to everybody else's horror, picked up the bread knife and plunged it deeply into Elizabeth back. Elizabeth turned in disbelief, stared wide eyed before slumping forward across the table amongst the crockery and the remnants of the meal. At that most inopportune moment, the air-raid siren sounded and the group were for once speechless and devoid of an immediate response. Which was more necessary - to run for the local tube station, or do something about Elizabeth. Up to that moment nobody had even checked that she was dead, though her inert and twisted body seemed to indicate that to check was merely a formality. Helen, however, was now crying and clinging on to Elizabeth's leg, having sensed that something was amiss, and finding her mother's lack of response to her crying and tugging unusual, and therefore unnerving.

Still nobody moved. Eventually, it was Maggie herself - since she had carved out for herself an important role as the Organiser and Shop Steward 'down the shelter' - who merely said to Beattie as she walked past her out the door, stepping around Elizabeth - who had now tumbled to the floor with her young daughter still pulling at her, and touching her face - "You done it. You fix it!"

Still nobody else moved, until Gladys turned eventually to Beattie, and slapped her smartly around the face, much to the surprise of her daughter, who was by now appalled at what she had done. They instructed her to gather up the children and follow her grandmother to safety, but Lena, Gladys and Connie remained. There was a lot of organising to be done.

They risked the air raid, discussing their best course of action. After the first real shock had died down, they had returned to their normal state of practical thought, not burdened with sorrow or remorse or any kind of responsibility. They decided that the air raid was a blessing. If they could discover if and where bombs had fallen they might be able to use any fatalities there as cover for their own inconvenient corpse.

When the all clear sounded, Connie went off to try and discover where, or if, a direct hit had occurred - it was strange even to her to consider the fact that she was hoping that this was the case. They could then weigh up their chances. It would be most convenient if damage had occurred somewhere close to, or on the way to, Elizabeth's own home. That would not only remove her from their locality, but would make more sense when she was found.

The rest remained at home, eventually re-joined by Maggie who was less than pleased that no real action had been taken to remove Elizabeth from under her kitchen table. When Connie came back with the news that a couple of houses had been hit, but they were not even close to either them, or Elizabeth's house, they sat up late into the night, trying to decide what was best to do. Eventually Maggie got fed up with all the talk and simply seemed to bring all the talking and hand-wringing to an end by firmly expressing the view that unfortunate as it was, and Beattie was obviously a stupid cow, it could not be helped. She was no loss anyway, and Jimmy was better off without her. Good riddance to bad rubbish, eh? Lots of good people were dying out there - good people, their people, English people. So, all they had to do was keep their heads, and decide where to move her to, and more importantly how to keep Beattie away from the law?

So, after dark, Gladys and Connie, using the old pram which was mostly nowadays used for washing, trundled the lifeless body of Elizabeth to a bomb-site where they left it, much to Connie's regret, but at Gladys's insistence, covered in the fur coat. In a show of final resentment and disrespect, and to vent her feelings at the 'stuck up cow' Gladys removed the dead woman's knickers, and ripped her much prized nylon stockings. Though Connie was reluctant to be a party to this, getting over her original distaste, she did realise that it could be a shrewd move. With a big knife wound in her back it could hardly be put down to Hitler! In any case it was some hours since the air raid, and even if there had been no damage close by, somebody would have found her before now when the air-raid wardens did their checks. That couldn't be helped now, but Connie had to admit that, though she realised it had not been Gladys's motivation - which was pure dislike - it could serve a useful purpose. It might look like some rapist or maniac had attacked her. She almost certainly would not be recognised and they were pretty sure they had not been seen, so nothing to tie her to them. Her bag with her ration book and anything else that identified her was still back at the house, so they were in the clear.

Unfortunately, they forgot to take back the pram, in their hurry to remove themselves from the scene. It was a very identifiable article -

having been bought from gambling winnings by one of the husbands, when he was feeling generous and perhaps hoping that he might at least curry a little bit of favour. The high-strutting baby carriage was decidedly more expensive and superior than anything else affordable in the locality and had raised many an eyebrow when it first appeared on the scene. It was not so pristine now, but was still recognisable for what it was, and sadly for them, whose it was. *(As far as the toadying husband was concerned, needless to say, his generosity had done him no real good).* The pram had long since been relegated to the chore of carting and carrying goods, rather than infants. It was now used principally by Maggie who often earned extra income by operating a successful laundry service downstairs in the basement of the house where the old boiler was often billowing out steam and belching out disapproval.

Off course or street betting - that is entrepreneurs earning money from horse and dog betting not carried on legitimately at the track itself - was illegal in those days. This provided another avenue for Maggie to earn a little bit of money and at the same time exercise her personal right to flout the law, and to inject a bit of excitement into her by then fairly uneventful life. When she returned the washing to its various owners, she would collect and deliver betting slips en route, together with the necessary financial stakes - and sometimes, albeit it very much the exception rather than the rule - deliver the winnings to the lucky few. Maggie, typical of many born in the East End of London from a long line of those used to 'making ends meet', was a canny rogue, smart and fearless.

At other times, if 'strange' bookies or their runners started operating in the neighbourhood, Maggie would sit at her window, and with no conscience at all alert the local beat bobby to their presence and their movements. She would get rid of the opposition, and the policeman would get a pat on the back for diligence and for a successful 'collar'. It was a mutually reciprocal arrangement since it also meant that he turned a blind eye to her nefarious wheelings and dealings.

But back to the pram!
Finding it on the bomb-site, the local children took a fancy to the pram and they were using it more or less in the fashion of a go-kart dragging it up the hilliest road they could find, putting some plucky or misfortunate child in it, and launch it off on its perilous journey to meet with a convenient patch of flat, albeit debris-strewn, waste ground at the bottom. This site had once, pre-bombing, been a handsome gable-end house, occupied by a dentist and his music teacher wife. Both had been killed in the direct hit, together with

the wife's mother and two pedigree Pomeranians. *(The building had obviously never been a lucky or safe place to be, since even prior to its final demise, it had been hit twice by lightning and once an unfortunate and distraught pregnant woman had used its garden wall, which abutted a steep drop onto a railway line, as a route to ending her own and her unborn baby's life).*

A local spiv, black-market racketeer, (or entrepreneurial wheeler dealer, according to whether you were Maggie and her family or not) who had over the years had on many occasions done business with them, saw the boys with the pram and recognised it immediately. He confiscated it, with a shark clip around the ear for several of the lads who tried to protect their new acquisition, and much to Maggie's outward show of gratitude and relief, but inward annoyance and trepidation, returned it to its rightful owners. He naturally told them how he had come across it, but Maggie was careful not to quiz him too much, though she would dearly have loved to know who the boys were, what else they might know.

They were perhaps even worse off now. It was very unfortunate that the pram had been identified. Even if there had been no mention of a body, or police, or anything untoward in the tale told by its retriever, the family lived from then on waiting for a knock on the door. In truth some of them were not sure whether they were most fearful that the knock would be the police, or the ghost of Elizabeth, or maybe worse still, Jimmy returning.

For a long time, nothing happened and they got more comfortable with the situation and were even congratulating themselves that despite Elizabeth, they had got Helen (obviously now called Nellie) and here she was, living with her cousins, as was only right. They had always done it that way. It was the custom.

They had written to Jimmy and informed him that Elizabeth had disappeared. She had turned up at their door, in a new fur coat, left Nellie with them, and cleared off. That had been in June (this was now September) and they had no idea where she had taken herself off to - probably returned to Ireland. They said that he was not to worry because they had his daughter safe and sound, so all was well. Jimmy was decidedly unconvinced by this information. He himself had received a letter from Elizabeth, for his birthday on the 13th June, and she had sounded her usual self, gave happy news of Helen, and said that, as she had promised, she was keeping in touch with his mother and sisters and was bringing Helen to see them. She had also commented that she was only doing this for his sake because they were still harping on about Helen going to live in Percival

Street, and as he knew there was absolutely no way that was going to happen - she had actually said 'over my dead body'.

Elizabeth had also included in her letter a note wishing him well from Mrs Greenberg, and a photograph. The photograph showed the two of them, together with a pipe-smoking Maurice Greenberg, standing in the garden, showing off Elizabeth's new fur coat. Marlys Greenberg in her note had said 'that old sable looks far better on your Elizabeth, than ever it did on me'. After the war, she said, 'it should be worth a bit of money, which might come in useful to get you all back on your feet'.

Jimmy had never been one to be melodramatic and he found it impossible to take seriously the thought that anything really untoward had happened to his wife. He was sure there was a logical and perfectly innocent explanation. Nothing could have happened to her! She had the whole family to look out for her. His mother was one of the shrewdest women he knew. No, Elizabeth was perfectly safe - apart from bloody Hitler's bombs, of course. That was a worry, of course it was. In some ways they were in a more dangerous situation than he was. Out here it was almost boring in comparison! Nothing but bloody thieving apes and permanently waiting around - almost going places, but never quite getting there! They had almost got to Greece - but had to turn back when it fell to the Gerries! Bloody fiasco that was! So life for him seemed at worst unpredictable - but not, as far as he could see, precarious! London, on the other hand, was being bombed constantly. But if something had happened to her - a direct hit, an accident, or an illness, or something, that would explain her leaving Helen - why had the family not been informed? None of it made any sense! It was definitely against every known fact and likelihood that she would up-sticks within a short space of time after that letter, take herself off and more importantly leave their daughter with them. Also, far from hiding some guilty secret about the coat, he knew exactly, from Mgrs. herself, that there was nothing dodgy about her being given the coat. Anyway, Elizabeth had seemed more than anything anxious that he should return and that they could go out together so she could wear it properly.

Eventually, trying to rationalise the conflicting information, he reluctantly reached the conclusion that Elizabeth must have had an accident. Perhaps with bombs falling on London she had been killed, or lost her memory, or was lying in an hospital bed somewhere unidentified, unconscious. Worse still, her body could be lying unidentified and unclaimed somewhere. That he now considered the more likely scenario - albeit still horribly distressing.

His family knew absolutely everybody in the vicinity and would have made enquiries, Elizabeth would surely have had identification of some kind on her when she was hurt and taken to the hospital - or worse. She must have been out of the neighbourhood - perhaps something had happened to one of her sisters and she had travelled to see them - she might easily have left Helen with them for a short while then - that would make sense. She had intended to be back quickly, but something had happened to her in the meantime - some kind of accident or a bombing somewhere away from home?

He had no idea how close he was to the mark. She was lying unnamed and unclaimed somewhere, though he was misguided in his assumption that it was an accident, whether pure mishap or bomb-related. He was also misguided in his assumption that his family would be moving heaven and earth to find her. The last thing they wanted was for her to be found - and worse still identified!

Months passed, and the family became more at ease and no longer worried about strangers coming to the door. After the birth of her new baby (a girl, Susan Margaret - obviously Susie) Beattie had been packed off to join the Land Army (much against her will) and was paying her penance knee deep in mud and animal shit in Lincolnshire. She was not happy, but as they pointed out, the alternative would be much worse, since unprovoked murder was likely to bring with it the death penalty.   She surely would rather be shovelling earth than buried six feet deep beneath it!

Chapter 4: The lull before the storm

When the war ended, though her family had tried to dissuade her from returning, suggesting that she might try a new life elsewhere - Australia, Canada, somewhere, anywhere - Beattie could not be dissuaded from re-joining her family and more especially retrieving her role as mother to Susie. She had been cocooned in her agricultural backwater and so it seemed to her that everything had died down. She had all but forgotten the 'incident' and could not imagine why they were being so negative about her coming home. She would brook no argument and despite their coaxing, cajoling and demanding, home she came, much to the disappointment of her grandmother, her mother and her aunts.

An uneasy normality returned to Percival Street until, as was inevitable, eventually a few months after the end of the war, a sceptical and thoroughly suspicious James did return. He had made as many enquiries as he could, via the Red Cross, to see if they could track down Elizabeth, but he got very little information. They had plenty other more deserving cases to solve - not to spend their meagre resources tracking down a woman who had probably just got fearful or fed up and skedaddled back home. He might have romanticised notions about the unlikelihood of her leaving her young daughter, but they had seen stranger things than that many times before. To make matters worse, he had contacted her sisters, one had not replied - though for all he knew she might have been killed too, since she had been living in Birmingham or Coventry or somewhere in the Midlands, and they had apparently had awful bombing raids too. The other one had replied, but was obviously also at her wits end. She had not heard from Elizabeth since June either. She was casting all kinds of wild accusations about his family, which was unnerving, but he still could not bring himself to believe his family capable of lying about her disappearance, let alone anything more sinister. He realised that Eileen, Elizabeth's sister, must be worried and jumping to conclusions.

So he had never taken such accusations seriously. After all, who would! His family were formidable women, but they were would not really going to do any real harm to anyone - and definitely not to a family member; not to his wife! But still, Elizabeth was missing.

She had, apparently, been missing since the Summer - that was months ago, so he was in no mood to leave it like that. He was depressed and even more upset by the unfortunate fact that Helen did not seem to know him - or worst still, take to him, at all.

At first there was merely an undercurrent which pervaded the house, with everybody seeming to walk on eggshells - a far cry from the outspoken, almost aggressive conversations that had taken place before the war. He had accepted that his daughter was decidedly uncomfortable around men in general, having seen precious few of them during her entire life time. Try as he might to accept as logical what he kept being told, namely that he was bound to be a stranger to her; she had never seen him before; things would improve; he needed to give her time, it was still very upsetting and added appreciably to his distress.

Helen seemed to be a very solemn little girl. Though she was not 'difficult' she was not only distant from him, but was always on the periphery of any games with the other children, and was silent and unsmiling most of the time.

Helen's reaction to her father merely seemed a kind of shyness, a failure to respond or come near him. She was, though, not just passive around Beatrice. She became positively angry when she was around. Still not vocalising her anger, but her face became distorted and she froze to the spot. One Sunday afternoon, when most of the family were present and Beatrice had insisted on trying to pick the little girl up and squeeze her so tightly that she was unable to wriggle free, Helen had bitten her with some vengeance on the shoulder and had kicked out, forcing the woman to release her grip. The child's sudden fury had taken them all by surprise. For that moment not the silent, watchful, sad little girl but a veritable spitfire - a cauldron of anger and hostility.

The women in the room, may not have had any formal qualifications, but they were all, in their own way, experts in human nature and human behaviour. They had used it to their advantage for a very long time one way and another. They, were only too well aware of the scenes that this little girl had witnessed not so very long before and the effect that that could have had on her. James on the other hand was merely dumbfounded! He became deeply worried that his small daughter was in some way emotionally, or even mentally, damaged. Which she was, but he had no idea why, or if he had he was not allowing himself to believe or countenance it.

Everybody started to bustle around finding useful things to do and reasons to leave the room.

As James read the newspaper later that afternoon, quietly sitting at the kitchen table, he was certainly surprised when his mother came in and asked, in quite an aggressive manner, when he thought he might be returning home to his own house. This was a very odd turn up for the books. Previously he had been the golden child, the apple of his mother's eye, so in both shock and something akin to anger he replied that he would go, if she wanted him out, as soon as he could make arrangements for somebody to look after Helen while he was at work. His mother was startled by this reply, and immediately said that there was no need for Helen to go anywhere, that she was perfectly happy where she was, and that they could continue to look after her, and he could pop in when he could. She would be perfectly fine, as she had been all this time.

Something, some bit of obduracy, got into him, and he told his mother that Elizabeth had never wanted Helen to be with anybody but her parents, and now that the war was over, he was determined to fulfil her wish. If he went, then Helen went too.

"That bloody woman again" was Maggie's response. "She was a bloody nuisance alive, ..." Suddenly realising what she was saying Maggie turned sharply on her heel and left the room, knowing that damage had been done, but not sure that any amount of continued conversation would redeem the situation. If they had to come clean, then they would. It was unlikely that her son, however much bewitched by that bloody Irish cow, would inform on his own niece and cause that amount of upheaval and dishonour to the family.

It was somewhat unfortunate for Maggie that the next person to come into the room was Beattie, who was still feeling aggrieved at the embarrassment of an actual attack on her by the four-year-old.

"Right little spitfire you have got there, Jimmy. Proper little Irish temper. I'm surprised she has not got bright red paddy hair! You sure she's yours! None of the other kids in the family have gone off their rocker like that one!"

"Mind your manners and your tongue, Beatrice. Show some understanding for a little girl who has lost her mother, and whose father has missed the first three years of her life."

"And what a mother, eh! Parading around here in a bloody fur coat, like Lady Muck. Got it from that Jew boy fancy man of hers, I dare say! You sure that little spitfire is not a Yid too?"

James went to raise his hand, but was stopped in his tracks when Beatrice suddenly said "Go on, put up a fight! More than your stupid Irish whore did when I gave her what was coming to her! Coming here upsetting everybody, upsetting my grandmother like that …. who did she think she was!"

It took a minute or two for what she was saying to filter through into James's brain, and then, coupled with the unfinished sentence in the last conversation with his mother, he saw only too clearly what had happened. He slumped into a chair, just as Maggie, Connie and Gladys all rushed in from various directions to see what the shouting was about. They saw a triumphant Beattie still standing hands on hips face suffused with anger, delighted with herself for putting Jimmy in his place.

"That's enough Beattie" said her mother. "Go and see what the children are up to."

James immediately reacted to that and said "Keep her away from my daughter. But get her out of my sight before I strike her dead on the floor. I never hated the bloody Germans the way I hate her, so believe me if I could bring myself to kill them, I can definitely lay her out, you had better believe it!"

Despite his mother, and his sisters trying to dissuade him, James immediately went in, gathered up his completely hysterical daughter, as many of their belongings as he could and left the house. He had no idea where he was going, or what he was going to do, but action seemed a better alternative than despair or staying under the same roof as those …. What were they? Who were they? Apart from being the only family he had ever known …. had he ever really known them at all!

The die had been cast and both mother and son had embarked upon a road of no return - they would never speak again in Maggie's lifetime.

Chapter 5:   Trying to make the pieces fit

James returned to the rented house that he had shared with his wife, but as was only to be expected, no rent having been paid for quite a few months, there were now other people living there.   He was at a complete loss to know what to do. It was by that time late into the evening, and he was still carrying not only the bits of belongings that he had brought away from Percival Street, but also a very tired little girl.   James was relieved that she was tired, because for the first half hour of their walk she had screamed and kicked and it was remarkable that nobody had accosted him and accused him of kidnapping her.

As he stood, trying to decide what to do, an Irish voice brought him back to reality.   At first he turned relieved and delighted believing that it was Elizabeth and that he had somehow misread the situation back at the house.   But it was not her.   As it turned out, it was a neighbour who lived a couple of houses further on, and who recognised Helen.

"Can I help you?   Oh Lord, that is little Helen?   Why have you got hold of her?   Where's Elizabeth?"   Then, having studied his face for a moment or two, she suddenly said, "Thank God! They're all right! I have been really worried about them …You're James! I recognise you from your photograph and of course the wedding!

Lost a bit of weight - I guess that's what the army does for you, eh!"

James was relieved to find somebody who knew at least of him, but he was reluctant to go into any details about his wife's whereabouts, given that he was unclear of them himself. He was also anxious to talk with this woman, who, as a fellow countrywoman of Elizabeth and a neighbour, might be able to throw some light on at least some parts of the picture.

Eventually, since it was getting late and he was still carrying a by now sleeping Helen, the woman said "God Almighty what kind of eejit am I! Come on in, at least I can put on the kettle. Kevin, my old fella, is snoring in the chair in his vest, but if you can stand that sight, you're welcome to come in for a bit of a warm."

James had never been so glad to have an invitation into a stranger's house in his entire life, not only because he was cold, tired and fed up, but more because he was confused. He was clueless about what to do next and avid to pump this neighbour for any information she might have about Elizabeth and what might have befallen her.

Laying Helen carefully on an empty armchair, he sat himself at a kitchen table and watched the woman as she bustled about making tea and big doorsteps of soda bread and ham.

As he sat, now and then looking anxiously across to where his small daughter was sleeping, he tried to make sense out of what was not in any way sensible. As is only to be expected, it being a most unnatural thought that your own family have conspired to murder your wife, he was now beginning to re-evaluate and doubt his earlier conclusions. Surely it was impossible to believe that such a thing could happen - Beatrice was not a lunatic - or she had not been a lunatic when he went off to war. Lord knows what had happened after that. By the look of the city it had taken a terrible pounding, and that could have been a bit of a jolt even for the most stable person - and perhaps Beattie had never been quite that - but not violent, surely, not to kill somebody. There had to be another explanation. Could something have happened to Elizabeth's mother, or somebody back home, and she had to go? But to just leave Helen like that? Surely she would just have taken her with her?

"Now get that down you. You look famished altogether! What's the craic with you? Where the hell is Elizabeth - she vanished into the night - like some kind of mystery woman in a fillem!"

James was fairly reluctant to tell the tale, since it sounded, even to him, beyond belief, and before he launched off into any kind of lurid story of murder and mayhem, he surely needed to find out what this woman knew first. He realised that he could not keep thinking of her as 'this woman'. She must have name. That was a start.

He started off, then, with at least an attempt at a proper introduction process: "Yes, as you guessed, I'm James - a bit of a slimmed down version, not by choice, more by army rations - but perhaps all the better for that. Elizabeth was forever telling me I was getting flabby!"

Seeing the tears begin to well up in his eyes, his hostess said, in order to relieve the moment a bit "Well, let me say then that me, for my sins, was christened, would you believe, Mavourneen. I think me ma must have had a drop or two on the way to the church to think that one up. People call me Maeve, not only is it shorter, but it doesn't make me sound like I should be in some kind of Irish American movie with leprechauns, rainbows and pots of gold.

That's me ole fella over there snoring on the chair - Kevin, Kevin Clarkin. Maeve Clarkin, for me sins. How do you do!" She made a pretend shake hands motion with her right hand, bread knife still clutched in her left one. She realised suddenly that she had it there, and said "I'm not a homicidal maniac, I promise, just so used to doing twenty things at the same time - that's the craic when you've a houseful of permanent whirlwinds!"

She put the knife down carefully on the table, handle facing James. She grabbed it again suddenly, much to his surprise, as she laughed and said "God, there I go again …. crossed knives …. a row in the house, I can do without any more of those for the time being!" ….

Replacing the knife again on a more isolated part of the tablecloth, she laughed in an almost embarrassed fashion, as though she was making small talk and frightened of running out of topics, which those that knew her would know was just not possible for Maeve. She went on "I've known Lizzie for years - I was at school with her sister, Kitty, and it was me that pointed her in the right direction to get the tenancy two doors up."

James was glad to hear that Maeve was a long-time friend of Elizabeth, because that might make it more likely that she might have told her things - like that she was fed up and was thinking of leaving, or that she was ill and the doctor had said she might keel over somewhere with heart attack - anything, anything at all that might mean that Beatrice was just being sensationalist and trying to be the centre of attention, or had had some kind of mad episode. Some people thought they were Napoleon, or Jesus Christ. Perhaps Beattie thought she was …. she was … a …. James found that he could not even think the word, and immediately returned to start a different conversation with Maeve.

"Maeve, good to meet you! As you will realise, I'm just back after too long away avoiding German shells and bullets. Glad to be back, but …… "

Eventually he could hold out no longer and found himself asking point-blank "Maeve, do you know where Elizabeth is? Did she tell you that she had to go somewhere? She didn't mention by any chance that her mother or somebody was sick, did she?"

Maeve stared at him and suddenly realised just how upset he was and that he had absolutely no idea where his wife was. But unfortunately, neither did she!

"James, really, I haven't seen her for ages now. I last saw her about early summer - about last June, I'd say because she had been in the night before for a chat and to bring a card and present in for my Christine - she was 7. Anyway, I was going out my door just as she was leaving the house. She had Helen in the pram, and said she was going off to see her in-laws …. oh, I suppose that would be your family, wouldn't it? Anyway that was what she said."

"Did she have bags with her - or a suitcase or anything?"

"No, nothing. She had a bag of shopping on the pram - I think things she was taking for your mother - you know she had a friend who worked at the Home and Colonial and sometimes she was able to wangle a few extra items on the coupons to eke out the rationing. We had a bit of a joke because she was wearing the auld fur coat that Mrs. Greenberg had given her and she was …. maybe I should not say this … but she said that her sisters in law would be green with envy, but that she just wanted to wear it…. You'll probably know better than me that there was no love lost there! Families, eh! Who'd have them!"

"That coat, Maeve! It certainly did cause a stir with my sisters and nieces, I can tell you!"

"It was great gas! I was over there - in Golders Green at the Greenberg's - helping out - you know if they had lot of visitors, Lizzie would get me a bit of work over there, it was a bit of money, and very welcome. Anyway. It was right after they had heard that one of their sons - I am not sure which one - had been taken as a prisoner of war. As well, they had lots of people there - they always had people there, you know staying with them from Europe and that, but this was different. They had been using the house to celebrate one of the visiting boy's coming of age - what is it called, Bar Mitzvah, or something. It was a bit subdued, but Mrs. Greenberg was always one for trying to make life as best as she could for everyone despite how sad she must have felt herself.

"Well, apparently, Mrs. Greenberg was kind of relieved in a funny sort of way that the lad had been taken prisoner of war - for some reason she found that a safer option - I suppose I kind of see the logic - than him still being out there fighting. There was also another son, who was somewhere in North Africa I gather. Anyway. Mrs. G was in a bit of a mixed mood. Trying to be happy for the celebration; trying to be positive about the prisoner son, and terrified for the other one. She got a bit maudlin at one point, standing in the kitchen and chatting - she was not much of a chatter when there was extra 'staff' in, though Lizzie used to say that she was nice enough and friendly enough at other times. Anyway, she was saying how lucky Lizzie and me were to have had daughters and that they might never have any daughters-in-law, or grandchildren now, so that we should be grateful every day for what we had and treasure them above everything.

It was then that she said to Lizzie that she had something she wanted to give her. She said it would be useful for her after the war because it would be worth a bit of money and it would help her look after Helen' - at this point Maeve stopped, and looked a bit embarrassed - then she continued ... 'well, James, what she actually said was, if something happens to James, and you are left on your own with Helen, you will have something to sell. She went off and got a beautiful fur coat - I never saw the like, except at the pictures! She also gave her a brooch - a diamond and emerald brooch, shaped like one of those lilies with the long stem - real I think, though I'm not the one to really tell real from paste - but since it was from Mrs. G. I would expect it to have been kosher - perhaps not the right word, but genuine, then.'

So there it was. The story of the coat was not a mystery. Jimmy was also finding some comfort in the fact that the family had not mentioned the diamond brooch. He was sure that they would have used it in their letter as further proof that 'she was carrying on', and it was therefore likely that they had never seen, or found, it. If Beattie had done what she implied she had done - heaven forbid! - then she/they would definitely have searched for anything - anything valuable, and anything identifiable. For some reason he could not fathom, he felt relieved by the brooch and its absence from the scene.

James and Helen stayed with Maeve that night. The little girl was put to bed topping and tailing with Colette, Maeve's four-year-old. James did his best to sleep on a too-short sofa in the living room, once Maeve had unceremoniously rousted poor Kevin from his snoring rest on the cosy armchair in front of the fire. The poor man seemed to take this in surprisingly good grace, and shook hands formally with Jimmy, gathering up the sleeping Helen in his arms, at his wife's instruction, and kissing the little tot on the top of her carried her up gently and affectionately to lay her down with his own little girl.

James had the rest of the night to contemplate the future, and to worry about the past.

Chapter 6: Who sees one body amongst so many?

At this time, at the tail end and the aftermath of the war, there were obviously lots of unknown, unclaimed and even unfound bodies in London. Priorities were necessary, man-power was overworked and limited; investigative methods and opportunities were relatively primitive and ill-defined. The chances of Elizabeth's body ever being identified were small to non-existent. Maggie was fairly sure about that. She had been worried about the bloody pram - real stomach churner that was, turning up like that! But it seemed to have led to nothing untoward. She had thought afterwards that she should have taken responsibility for getting rid of the Irish witch's body herself - it had been too risky to leave it to the girls. She saw now, despite her order (delivered in a fit of pique) that since Beatrice had caused it, she should put it right, that in reality there was no way that they could have left it to that silly cow! The girls had been right about that. She was glad they had taken the initiative! Even when she got to the shelter that evening she had realised that she had been too hasty, and was quite glad - though she didn't let the girl know it - to see Beatrice turn up crying and carrying on, but shepherding the kids down the steps to safety. She just decided to hope for the best - and the girls had done good! They had managed all right - eventually! It was disconcerting to return home and find the corpse still lying under the kitchen table - not your everyday occurrence but she could see, when she had calmed down, that it would have been stupid to try to do anything at all before the air raid threat was past and before people had gone back to their homes and the streets were more deserted. She had heaved many a sigh of relief over the following months, and was glad that they were gradually getting back to business as usual.

Little did the family know that in a most unexpected and almost unbelievable quirk of fate, at the time the body was discovered, the air-raid warden who found it, was smart enough, lucky enough, and honest enough, to a) realise that the woman had been stabbed rather than killed by Hitler's bombers; b) find the coat still covering the body, with, of all things an expensive looking brooch in the pocket; and c) find these observations suspicious and report back to the appropriate authorities. Had she not had the coat and what turned out to be real diamonds, the state of her undress, would most certainly have led the police to believe that she was a street walker - a prostitute.

The conclusion drawn by the lower ranks was that this was a 'tom', a 'working girl'. However, the now ripped and ruined stockings spoke differently to the more senior and experienced detectives.

They were originally of very good quality and consequently very expensive. The valuable coat and exquisite jewellery had both passed muster, being both genuine, and as far as they could tell, never reported stolen. On such decisions is fate decided. Those having the responsibility opted to be more circumspect. If the victim was actually a woman of means rather than some poor cow who had met up with the wrong client, then somebody might have their guts for garters if they sidelined it. So despite there being plenty going on to occupy their minds, and despite it not being, by necessity, at the top of their agenda, it had still remained an 'open' (though more ajar than wide open) case for the Metropolitan police, with the body preserved and such evidence and witness statements kept in case further information - or claimants for the body - came to light. Most of those who had taken a cursory gander through the evidence were still inclined to think it 'a domestic' - which of course it was, but not quite in the way that the detectives had conjectured. They all expected the culprit to be 'the husband' - and knew that his money would buy him a good lawyer even if they found him. The missing underwear was just to make it look like a street crime. They weren't fooled!

So there was no speedy rush to investigate since nothing was normal or easy at that time. There were plenty of problems and concerns to keep such detectives busy and though they did not consciously ignore it, it was quite well down the list of priorities.

Eventually, when they did turn their mind to investigate it, they were inclined to stick with their first assumption, from the coat and the brooch, that the body was that of a well to do woman. It certainly had never entered into their minds that she was neither a wealthy murdered wife - or mistress - or a prostitute with a side-line in burglary. She was in service! A housekeeper, perhaps, but technically a servant nonetheless. Eventually then, when the case reached the top of the pile, the presumed status of the corpse had the effect of putting a bit more urgency into the investigation, though the brightest amongst them found it puzzling nonetheless that the expensive coat and the even more expensive brooch had not been taken away by whoever killed her. If it was her old man surely he must have known that if he was trying to make it look like a sex crime, that the coat and the bloody diamonds might be a bit of a liability!

They had then very early on formed the opinion that she had not merely been the victim of a mugging or killed in the course of a robbery. The wound in the back did not seem to indicate that she was facing her attacker, more that he had somehow stolen up behind her, or even deliberately waited for the right opportunity and driven some kind of blade into the unsuspecting woman. According to the Warden there did not seem to be any sign of a bloody pool or evidence of a fight or struggle. There were no defensive wounds and the blow itself was straight into her back, left of centre, and unfortunately for the victim, in direct line with her heart. It was difficult to see it having been inflicted other than with the victim standing with her back squarely away from her killer definitely not in self-defence or even spur of the moment.

The coat was the biggest clue. There was a very exclusive furrier's label sewn into the garment, which easily led them to the right tailor, and then on to the door of Mr. Maurice Greenberg, in Golders Green, North London. Obviously there first assumption was that the body was that of Mrs. Greenberg - for whom the coat had been bought some twelve years earlier at the time of her fifteenth anniversary.

Arriving at the house, however, the door was opened by a young girl, who, having shown them into an immaculately furnished and orderly drawing room, went off to inform 'Madam' that they were there.

Marlys Greenberg very quickly came in to speak with them, and since her husband and both her sons (now home safely and demobbed from their regiments) were both out and about, she feared that somebody had been injured or worse. Her face told that story as she joined them, and she introduced herself to them, asking them anxiously whether anything was the matter.

The two detectives, (George Stringfellow and Daniel Evans) had not expected to be greeted by the woman of the house, believing 'the woman of the house' to be the subject of their enquiries. This was obviously not a dollybird 'replacement' wife that one murdered the missus for! This woman was well into her 50s, smart, but not by any means a 'looker'! However, DS Evans pulled himself together quite quickly and explained that they were making enquiries about a body that had been found. They would be interested to know who might have had access to a sable coat, tailored in Whitechapel, by Messrs. Moskavitch, Klausen and Rubins, and purchased by her husband, Maurice Greenberg, in 1933?

By this time, they were beginning to assume that the coat - and probably the brooch - had been merely the proceeds of a robbery, and that they were wasting their time investigating the murder of a thief who had merely fallen out with her accomplice. But why had that accomplice not retaken the coat and brooch? Panic, presumably?

Marlys Greenberg was getting less anxious that something was amiss with her own family, but more concerned that something had happened to Elizabeth.

"I gave the coat - and a brooch, actually - to my former housekeeper, Elizabeth, some time ago. Her husband, James, was here only the other day, asking if I had seen her, or if she had said anything about going back to Ireland - he thought perhaps her mother or a relative was ill, or something. He seemed like he was clutching at straws, Detective, because he had already contacted her two sisters - I am not sure where they live - one is a cook, I know - Coventry, I think- and the other is a seamstress - one of the big fashion houses, but I don't know which one. I think it was in London somewhere but I think they might have moved out - East Anglia maybe? …. near the sea, I seem to remember, at least it looked like it from the photographs - I think, during the war. Now I am really shocked. Apparently she left her small daughter with her in-laws, and I know that she was most unlikely to do that unless something terrible had happened, or was about to happen. Oh My God, I do so hope - please no! - that it not is her!"

The detectives asked if she by any chance had a photograph of Elizabeth, and Mrs. Greenberg went over to a bureau by the large bay window, looking out onto a sweeping drive and pristine lawn, bordered by well-tended flower beds. She returned with a copy of a photograph very like the one that Elizabeth had sent to James, with the note from Marlys, explaining about the coat and the brooch.

And there **was** the coat, and indeed the brooch, with Elizabeth looking proud as punch and well and truly alive. That had been the previous June, according to Mrs. Greenberg.

The detectives made no comment directly to Marlys Greenberg, but each individually were able to identify for themselves the fact that Elizabeth Collier was, indeed, their victim.

Having taken their leave of Mrs. Greenberg, not indicating either way, whether the photograph matched their body or not, they returned to their car and sat for a few moments taking in what they had learned, and indeed what they had made of the information they had received.

They would need to find the husband, James Collier, wherever he might be. It was unlikely that he was responsible - what idiot would draw attention to his wife's absence like that, if he knew only too well what her fate had been! As well as that, Mrs. Greenberg had told them - though he may have lied to her, but it was easy to check - that he had been in the Army right through the war, and had only returned to the UK relatively recently. She had mentioned that he told her he had been in Gibraltar during June when he got the photograph - which was when the body had been found. So likely it was not him, but he would need to be found in any case. The army would probably have a record of his address - at least his whereabouts prior to the start of the war and his call up.

After a short while sitting in silence, DC Stringfellow, suddenly said "What about her husband?"

"You gone barmy, you daft Welsh git! We just had a bleedin' ten-minute rabbit about her bloody 'usband - …."

"No, I mean her husband" and he gesticulated towards the window of the Greenberg house.

Dan Evans was used to all the gibes and the mickey taking about him being from Wales. George Stringfellow was one of the better ones. At least he did it to everybody, and took it back in return. He was six feet seven, with enormous feet and hands - and was more often than not referred to as "Beano", from his likeness to a beanpole. Everybody in the station - probably everybody in the force below the rank of DI, and even them, behind their backs - was probably labelled with some derisory or descriptive tag, depending upon their birthplace, their hair colour, the size of their nose or anything else that presented their peers with a good handle to hang it on. Evans, as usual, ignored it, as his colleague knew he would, and continued as though it had never happened.

"Could he have been carrying on with the housekeeper? Funny things go on in these swanky houses, don't they? Or he could have just been bloody mad that his wife gave away his expensive anniversary present, not to mention a sodding diamond brooch!"

"Anything's possible, Dan, but wouldn't he have got back the coat and brooch? Seems a bit stupid - either way - really. The coat identified them, after all, and the brooch is worth a fortune. I don't really see him trolling up to Chalk Farm to stick a knife in the housekeeper's back himself - and if he had 'paid' somebody to do it - and that would be a bloody big risk in itself, laying yourself at some violent criminal's mercy - with those blackmail possibilities - surely the 'assassin' would have nicked the coat and the brooch. What scrote is going to leave them behind, eh!"

"I guess, you're right, Dan, it wouldn't make sense would it - but spur of the moment thing, or something?   Throes of lust or anger? She could have been stabbed anywhere and driven to that bomb-site, couldn't she?   People don't think straight when they are mad, sad or high as a kite?   For all we know he could be any one of those - we have only met her (again he nodded towards the Greenberg house).   Maybe we should try to see him as well - and the sons. Though from what seems likely - them being prisoners of war and that, they were probably not even in London then. Most of the troops, and definitely the POWs were not brought back until well after June.   Same alibi as James Collier himself, isn't it?"

With that, still watched from an upstairs window by a tearful Marlys, George put the car into gear and they drove away.   She was sure though they had not said so, that the 'body' was poor Elizabeth.

Chapter 7:   Trying to move on, without success.

With the help of Maeve, who seemed to know everybody, everything and all the right people, James had managed to find himself and Helen rented accommodation close enough to their previous home, to enable him to return to work, knowing that his daughter was being perfectly well looked after by Maeve.   Helen or Hell's Bells as Maeve tended to call her - which would have caused Elizabeth to turn in her grave - if she had one, rather than a cupboard in a morgue) was becoming slightly more relaxed and though still not an out-going and playful little girl, with Maeve's care and her father's patience and love, she was beginning to come out of her shell a little.

Kevin, too, was a natural with children - a big kid himself was the verdict of his adoring wife - and he always included Helen in any treat or outing he thought of for his own children.   Helen in turn loved being around Kevin which was helping her to feel more comfortable around men in general.   Their own children surprisingly never showed any jealousy or pique at this new child's constant inclusion and intrusion into the family.

Maeve and Kevin were a wonderful balm to soothe the anxieties and distress of both Helen and James.   Maeve had known Helen since birth, and her mother, and her mother's family and background, even before that, so was as good a surrogate as could be found.

Obviously everybody wished that such surrogacy was not necessary and that Elizabeth was still living amongst them, but failing that ideal, Maeve was definitely the next best thing. Maeve was able to help her to move on following the huge loss of her mother and the sudden arrival into her life of this man - this kind man, this gentle man - who called himself her 'Daddy' but whom she had never before seen. The most difficult thing for James's arrival into Helen's life was the fact that it came so inextricably linked with the removal of her mother from it - she went, he came! Her mother was loved, he was unknown, mistrusted and alien to everything the child had ever known. Little wonder that she considered that he was responsible in some way.

This obviously faded a bit over the years, but the person who slew her mother was responsible also for a deep gulf being created between a little girl and her father. A gulf that diminished and got replaced by acceptance and gratitude as she grew and realised that that too was not going to be taken away from her, but never quite went away altogether. She learned to hide it much better with time and with her mother's inherited acting skills but she was probably a very damaged little person, and the love, the care, the 'normality' that her poor father, and Maeve, and Kevin tried to heal her with were probably just a tourniquet stemming a flood of hurt, anger and vengeance.

Not only was there a glass wall between herself and those close to her, but that wall was not just glass, but reinforced concrete, between herself and everybody else. She remained forever a shell, a vacuum, to the rest of the world. She learned to say the right things, to smile or cry in all the right places, but in truth, Helen would have been perfectly at home in a waxwork - she looked like Helen, she talked like Helen, but she really felt nothing. Her entire emotional well-being had been destroyed. Destroyed by one person, but aided and abetted by the family. His family. Her family.

Chapter 8: A Successful Investigation

Following the visit to Golders Green and following up on the information given to them by Marlys Greenberg, the police obtained James's pre-war address from the Army records, but that proved a dead end, because, as we already know, new people had moved in some months before.

They now knew that he had been in Gibraltar for much of the latter months of the war, and in Scapa Flow before that. It was confirmed that he had had absolutely no opportunity to return home for a good long time prior to his demob. Without prompting, they were told that Private James Collier had an exemplary record. The supercilious bureaucrat answering their enquiries on behalf of the military, was incensed that they should suggest the possibility that their man might somehow have gone AWOL or managed to wangle a trip home on the quiet. They were left in no doubt that if they themselves had had any experience of life during a period of extreme hostilities, as his poor chaps had known through almost six years of horror and mayhem, they would know better than to suggest any such possibility! Did they think they were all on some kind of pleasure trip? Did they envisage that serving soldiers came and went as the mood took them? It was not some kind of boy scouts' jamboree that if you got home sick, they just gave you a lolly pop and sent you home! People - serving soldiers - did not just take off willy-nilly as and when the mood took them, on fancy flights home for a night of nooky!

Eventually they were able to extricate themselves from the ear bashing, but also with the confirmation that they had sought in the first place. So, likely it was not him, but he would need to be found in any case.

From marriage registrations they also found out that Elizabeth's maiden name had been Quinlan. They tracked down her sister, Hannah, who was living in Coventry. Her other sister had apparently returned to Ireland soon after the outbreak of war. Hannah had never married and had been employed in the same household for several years.

From the photograph, she was able to identify Elizabeth, and was also able to give them the new address for James and Helen. She told them that she had received a letter from her brother-in-law, while he was still overseas with the army - she was obviously not sure where overseas, because that kind of information was always hush-hush - asking her if she knew of any relative being ill or dead at home in Ireland that Elizabeth might have gone to visit or assist with.

She had not replied - she had meant to, but ... well she knew for certain that there was no crisis or problem at home that had called her sister back. If that was the case, she herself, as the oldest sister, would have probably known first. If that was true, then apart from Elizabeth choosing to make herself scarce - from James's family, if not from him - then she had no explanation that she could tell him. She just kept putting off replying until it seemed too late.

The detectives were sceptical. Surely she must have been concerned herself? If she was certain Elizabeth had not returned home, and her sister was to all intents and purposes missing, then it was very suspicious that she did nothing, contacted nobody, just, as she said, 'kept putting it off'.

When pushed, she admitted that she was surprised, that Elizabeth had left Helen behind. She had never been particularly anxious to be a mother, but she had always had a tremendous sense of duty and respectability. She would no more have wished to be looked upon as shirking in her parenting duties than she would have left James for another man. It was just not in her nature.

No, definitely her sister had absolutely never mentioned anybody else - it was ludicrous - she was prudish, squeamish almost, about any kind of intimacy - she was not even a very touchy feely person - never had been.

The detectives pushed her again on the possibility of a new man in her life, with her husband away, and …. well these things happen.

Hannah looked scandalised!   No, no, no!   It was impossible!   She stopped and stared at them before continuing …. repeating her assertion, but adding that even if her belief was totally mistaken and Elizabeth had been bowled over by some mad passionate love affair (and that was so laughable as they would realise if they had ever known her sister!) she would absolutely never, never, never have just up sticks and gone without taking her child.   Elizabeth was above everything concerned about appearances, about respectability.   She just would not have done it!

Neither Stringfellow nor Evans were inclined to accept all this as proof positive that Elizabeth Collier had not just gone off with a fancy man, regardless of the views of her sister.   She would say that wouldn't she?   With her up in Coventry and Elizabeth down in

London, who knew how the woman had changed - There she was, footloose and fancy free with Jimmy Collier off in the army, saddled with a child. She had to stop working so was at a loose end. With her new coat and diamond brooch, who knew how that might turn even a prude's head! She would not be the first, and almost certainly not the last, wife to have strayed. They did not say any of that and stood up to leave.

However, before they could take their leave, amongst floods of tears born of self-recrimination and worry, long-bottled up and stifled, Hannah volunteered that she had had a second letter from James, now that he was back in England, enclosing a photograph of her niece, and asking her if she still had not heard from his wife.

She had still been too embarrassed to reply and admit that though she had not heard from her sister, she had done absolutely nothing about it. Hannah was by that time concerned and afraid that something had indeed happened to her sister, but she was also afraid to make a big fuss. There were thousands of people missing. She was Irish, and the police had enough to do without bothering with her. In any case, she could lose her job if she was responsible for too much intrusion or publicity for her employer's family, and she had decided to leave the searching to James, and just pray that her sister was safe and well and would turn up somewhere.

The investigating officers were appalled by this reaction, and a tearful Hannah explained that though she probably sounded unfeeling this was just one more cross for her to bear. She had originally been the second eldest of 13 children - with nine surviving past infanthood. Now there were only three left. The rest had been lost to wars, to accidents, even three lost crossing to America when their ship was hit by a torpedo. And now Elizabeth. Death and loss had become part of her life. They must forgive her if she sounded resigned and unmoved.

It was clear the officers were somewhat unconvinced by Hannah's attitude and acceptance, and but for the fact that she had been hospitalised as a result of an air-raid which totally devastated the property which backed onto the house in which she was employed as a cook more or less at the time in June when her sister's body was found, she would have gone right to the top of their 'suspect list'. With her 'alibi' checked, the officers were left, however, believing that perhaps the Quinlan family were perhaps more than a little bit jinxed!

With the new address, eventually James was interviewed and formally told of his wife's fate. That presented him, as his mother had known it would, with a dilemma. He knew he could not pretend even to himself that he had not suspected the truth. Beatrice had all but spelled it out. His mother too had said as much. They had known all along. But it was not going to bring Elizabeth back by getting Beattie punished. It would make it more traumatic, not less. James had a real dilemma on his hands. Did he lose permanently his entire family - which he had probably lost anyway, since nobody had been in touch, or tracked him down, since he left his mother's house with Helen - in order to punish them for Elizabeth's death? Did he know for absolute certainty that they were responsible? Would it bring Elizabeth back? Would it be just another burden for Helen to carry? Oh God! What had Helen seen on that day? What did she remember? She was only tiny, but such memories stayed deep inside a person's head and …. could that be why she was so withdrawn, so unreachable? He decided that since he now believed, as far as Helen was concerned, the likelihood was that the damage had already been done, he would tell the police all he knew - well perhaps not all he KNEW, but at least all that he suspected. To hell with the consequences, and if he stayed alone and without kith and kin from now to eternity, then so be it. It was for Elizabeth, and even more for Helen, who now faced growing up not only without a mother, but also a deeply damaged and benighted little girl.

Chapter 9: The truth, the whole truth and nothing but the truth: more or less; give or take!

Finally, the dreaded knock came to the door and loyalty, family, kinship and courage were all put to the test - and to the sword.

When the whole episode was eventually pieced together, though Maggie sanctioned against it, and cautioned them all to stand together and say nothing, admit nothing, offer nothing, the terrified family turned on itself, and named Beattie as the perpetrator, though carefully and deviously being less honest and clear about the where, why, when and how. Beatrice, on the other hand, obeyed instruction from her grandmother, and kept the family out of it, as much as she could. She let it be thought that she had met up with Elizabeth by chance, and an argument had ensued because Elizabeth had taken exception to the fact that she was pregnant and unmarried, and that she was making a show of the family. Elizabeth, was Roman Catholic, devout, and very prudish. She had looked down on Beatrice for ages and had told her that she would not let Nellie live there because she was a trollop and a flirt. She - and her bastard child - would be a bad influence on her own daughter and she did not want to be associated with their tarnished reputation. Maggie had indeed rehearsed her well. Beatrice did as she was told. The police had their killer and needed to investigate no further. No reference was ever made to any involvement the rest of the family might have had in the death, or its covering up. It was decided to try Beatrice for the death of Elizabeth Collier, her aunt. Had the family not thrown Beatrice to the wolves, and had her grandmother in particular not left her with no alternative but to own up to it, albeit with mitigating circumstances, it may well not have got that far, since there were no other witnesses to the event, and no other motive could be identified, apart from Beatrice's own admission and her claim that she had ultimately reacted to Elizabeth Collier's constant verbal and physical attacks.

Though it was obvious to all attending the trial, or reading about the case in the papers, that there was something not ringing true and the general feeling was that the woman could not have acted alone. What was never really challenged during the investigation - which, after getting the confession from Beatrice, was cursory at best was why there was so little evidence of the killing at the scene; how did she just happen to have a long bladed knife with her at the time; why was it necessary to stab the victim in the back? There were many who were of the opinion that she must surely have been aided and abetted, but no attempt was made to establish or prove this, and no mention was made of anybody else, either by Prosecution or Defence. As to what Elizabeth was doing on a bomb-site nowhere even close to home, without her underwear, nobody seemed to find it necessary to enquire. So the case that went to trial worked on the same assumption that everybody else had been allowed to believe - that Beatrice had met with, and stabbed Elizabeth where she was found. Needless to say, none of the family stepped forward to shed any other light on the matter, so she alone was deemed to be involved in what the Prosecution tried to label as this 'act of barbarity and viciousness', whereas the Defence, naturally, portrayed the whole sad episode as an act of sadness and tragedy at a time in her life when his client was at her lowest ebb, with a war raging around her, a fatherless child in her belly, and an aunt who not only called her a slut and a fallen woman, but also flaunted a fur coat and diamond brooch in her face. To a young woman who had nothing, and nobody, this was a barb too far and she acted, quite out of character and in a way that she thoroughly regretted and would regret for the rest of her life.

It had to be remembered, he said, that anybody could have come along after the event - the body was not found for several hours - and removed the underwear. There are some very unsavoury - perverted people - out there. *(It was not the Defence Counsel's job to remind jurors and the Judge that this same perverted or unsavoury character - or even a savour, but dishonest one - could have/would have taken the fur coat!)* The defendant had not intended to kill, even to harm. The attack was out of character and completely unpremeditated - the result of stress and pregnancy and the continual castigation by Elizabeth Collier, who had been welcomed into the family home and treated as a sister. Beatrice Collier was not denying that she had unfortunately killed her relative by marriage, but it was not a cold blooded, calculated murder, and it was an unfortunate, and much regretted, outcome of the torment that his client had suffered and her dire circumstances, being pregnant, alone, and surrounded by war and devastation.

The jury were reluctantly forced to find the case proved, since Beatrice had admitted the charge, and only the mitigating circumstances were actually on trial, though they had served her quite well.

Summing up, the judge, Judge Gerald Cathcart, considered that though she had plunged the knife, Beatrice herself was the victim of an upbringing and environment which was deeply flawed. He seemed to commiserate with her and suggest that the murder of Elizabeth was the result of a sudden aberration - a kind of fit of pique almost. *An embarrassed murmur went around the courtroom and a sharp in-taking of breath was heard in the public gallery at his words. The word 'pique' seemed quite alien and 'foreign' to the ears of the down to earth spectators.   Surely 'pique' described a bit of a paddy, a bit of foot stamping, a mild temper tantrum, rather than a fit of anger, rising to violence, and culminating in the death of a young wife and mother.   The stir was palpable, and it caused some movement and reaction from the ushers and Court officials.*

There were also a few people also in the public gallery who, though feeling somewhat embarrassed, also added in their own minds "who had done nothing to warrant it, apart from preferring to have her own child live with her".

From my interviews with Gladys some years down the line, I know that there were one or two - not least, strangely, Maggie, the architect of the piece, and Gladys herself, the mother of the culprit - who were affected by the trial in a way that was both sobering and thought-provoking.   It had a deep and profound effect on Maggie, who never really recovered, and her change in demeanour and leadership eventually drove away both Lena and Connie, though Gladys remained with her to the end.   Strangely it was not the verdict that was the cause of her change of heart, but the sudden understanding that the whole episode had been brought to a head because of her insistence that her grandchildren should live with her.

She had insisted on this for a reason she had never divulged to anybody, and now that very insistence had brought about the very thing - and worse - that she had sought to avoid.

She knew - as did all of the family - that her daughter-in-law had never commented or chastised Beatrice for her pregnancy, or her behaviour. She, Maggie, had herself thought up that strategy and had schooled Beatrice well in its delivery. She had been lost in her own thoughts, regrets and forebodings so was oblivious to Judge Cathcart's final words before he closed the trial and went on to sentence Beatrice for her crime.

"and constantly criticising her niece for letting the family down by being unmarried and of low moral character!! Such barbs may be treated as water off a duck's back by us, the educated, the well-respected, the stable, but to somebody of this young woman's ilk, it was more than she could bear."

Sensing the disapproval of some of his audience, because of his previous poor choice of vocabulary, and his obvious bias towards the perpetrator and away from the victim, Judge Cathcart tried to counteract some of the hostility, acknowledging completely that an act of aggression had occurred and a visitor to this country was now dead and lost to her husband and daughter. It showed a poor view of England to the rest of the world, and such an act must, therefore, carry consequences. The law was clear. It was an unprovoked attack - physically that is - but it seemed to have been completely unpremeditated and was perpetrated by a very young woman, in a delicate condition, facing great worries and recriminations; a young woman from a family whose whole fabric seemed to be one of verbal abuse and underlying menace. It was a set of circumstances that was hard to ignore, both the crime itself, and the factors leading up to it.

The judge peered around the courtroom, and more pointedly at the gallery, letting his gaze sweep around the entire expanse, before continuing. "But obviously a crime has been committed, and a woman, a visitor to our country, is dead and though obviously the crime was unpremeditated and I am sure the defendant is remorseful, that fact cannot be ignored."

Beatrice was found guilty of the unpremeditated killing of Elizabeth Collier, her aunt by marriage.

Deciding on the sentence, the Judge seemed to be swayed by the following factors: the woman was not local, that is not a British citizen; she was an Irish national; the defendant's own grandfather had been traumatised by the war in Ireland, and was still suffering with his nerves and suffering episodes of distress following those times and the family had been badly affected by this; the crime had taken place during what everybody knew had been a most traumatic and difficult period for all - the war was still raging and bombs were falling; nobody could fail to be affected and almost everybody was acting out of character in some way or another because of the terrible events happening around them; moreover, and above that, Beatrice was in a very delicate frame of mind due to the pregnancy and her own unmarried state. These were all factors that could not be ignored.

In addition, there was little information available with regard to any other motive apart from - what seems to a rational person - to be a very flimsy one, namely the verbal criticism. It was difficult to believe that this young woman had deliberately set out to kill somebody with no rhyme or reason behind it.

Though one should not rise to verbal attack or derision, she had found it difficult to not get angered by her aunt's criticisms and taunts when she was so concerned and in such a dark place. As for the victim, who knew what made her provoke her young niece so cruelly. She - the deceased - had led a very difficult life; she was considerably older than the defendant, her husband was - like many others - away at war, she was a mother for the first time at an advanced age. Nobody was in a position to really say what had happened in those minutes immediately before the incident.

All of the above, makes me believe that this young woman is as much sinned against as sinning and despite the need to prescribe an appropriate and adequate sentence to acknowledge that a person is dead, I also believe that some kind of psychiatric report is required so that the penalty paid takes into consideration the future mental health of the Beatrice Collier, as well as the safety of the rest of society.

So all these factors, both accepted and dismissed, persuaded the Judge to be lenient. Much to the family's astonishment - and indeed delight - he decided that it had not been proven to his satisfaction that the young woman had gone out deliberately in order to take the life of her aunt. (*No challenge or explanation was ever asked or offered for Beatrice having had a broad-blade 'bread-type' knife with her when she met Elizabeth*). There were absolutely no witnesses available to say exactly what had happened; no valuables had been taken - indeed the very coat that identified the victim was left at the scene and her jewellery - including a diamond brooch worth a lot of money were still with the corpse. It had not been a case, therefore, of this defendant choosing to kill in order to rob the victim. Neither was there anything to argue against the contention that the defendant had just been taken by a sudden fit of fear or uncharacteristic panic.

He decided that Beatrice should be assessed by a psychiatrist before he decided upon a sentence, since he believed, given her delicate state, she may have been anything but thinking rationally when the incident occurred. *(I was not called upon to work on Beatrice's case, since I was at that time relatively junior in status, which happily meant that I was free to be called upon to work in due course with her cousin Helen some 13 years later.)*

Eventually when reports had been submitted and Beatrice, who had been very well schooled by her grandmother over many years of wheeling and dealing, had worked her magic and cried the necessary tears, the psychiatrist considered that she had been under intolerable stress at the time of the incident, and that she had acted out of character. The Judge therefore decided that though a term of imprisonment was probably required, given that a life had been lost, he decided upon a term of 15 years, with no minimum sentence, leaving it to the discretion of the prison authorities to decide whether parole, after a suitable period, would be a humane decision, so that she could be allowed to have at least some time with her young daughter while she was still a child.

As James sat in the gallery, unable to repudiate any of these calumnies against his wife, or to give any real witness account to negate them, he was horror struck by the duplicity of his own family.

He knew the facts to be probably almost entirely concocted - probably by his mother - he could give no witnessed account of any alternative, apart from gut feeling and hearsay. Not being a witness, he was not called by the Prosecution. His 'hearsay' account of what his niece and his mother had said, would just muddy the water, and serve no useful purpose.

Returning home at the end of the proceedings, and sitting around Maggie's kitchen table, mugs of tea steaming before them, the bigger mystery was discussed. Why had nobody pinched the bloody fur coat during the time that it lay on the bomb-site! If they had, then Elizabeth would probably never have been identified and all would have been well. Needless to say, hindsight being a wonderful thing, if they had known that it was possible for a fur coat to be identified by its labelling, then they would have burned the bleedin' thing - although that would have been a terrible waste and would have gone very much against the grain! And to think they also missed a bleedin' diamond brooch. They must be losing their nose! That was, though, one of the last times that the family sat congratulating themselves on their partial victory or laughing at their faux pas. Each, for their own reasons, felt dissatisfied by the outcome. Two of them were thrown and let down by failure on the part of Maggie who had not been able to wave a magic wand and make it all go away. She had let them down. She was not all powerful after all. Lena and Connie from then on - much to their husbands' misfortune - spent much more time at home ruling their own roost and keeping their own families in order. They visited their childhood home occasionally but despite no actual words of separation ever being uttered, both they and Maggie understood the parting of the ways and both sides were comfortable with the situation.

Gladys alone remained, with her other children, spending most of her time with her mother, until Maggie's death, awaiting the eventual return of Beatrice.

PART TWO

Chapter 10: There are always consequences: Helen's Story

James was eternally grateful for the generosity, support and sometimes superhuman understanding and patience of Kevin and Maeve during those first desperate and faith-sapping months.

Through her many 'contacts' and because of her friendship with all and sundry - regardless of race, creed, sex or personality - there was not much that Maeve did not know or hear, not only around the immediate locality, but also somehow far and wide. Through this 'gift' she was able after a few days to identify a third of a three storey house that James could rent, which was close enough to her own home in order to make it possible for her to look after Helen when James was at work - and not infrequently other times as well.

James loved Helen dearly, but he was no great shakes at the more basic skills of parenting, finding the responsibility of looking after and cosseting a small, and frequently taciturn, little creature a bit of a puzzle. He meant well, and was quick with a kiss, a cuddle and a new toy. The more day to day responsibilities - like getting her washed, dressed and ready to face each and every day, then bathed, undressed and settled down each and every night was a routine he found difficult to master, like many another man even in a two-parent family! The sheer monotony was difficult for him, as was the loneliness and responsibility of it all. He missed Elizabeth, not only for her wit, her charm and her never stinting support when he was down, but he missed, too, her ever-practical role, as wife, mother, cook, house cleaner and money earner.

In truth, secretly, he could never really be sure which of those aspects he missed the most, but that did not make him a callous or selfish man. It made perfect sense and was unavoidable. His now dead wife had been the driving force, the planner, the 'doer', the putty that kept the windows in place. She had prevented the world intruding or harming. She had protected them from the unexpected, the unwelcome. To put it in a nutshell, James was completely out of his depth. Much worse, he had been forced to face the fact that ultimately she had not been able to protect herself - and he had not been there to save her from his family: From her family!

Under other circumstances, a man would be able to turn to his own family. Under other circumstances how simple that would have been! They were almost all female, healthy, practical, accomplished homemakers, child-rearers, strategists. But these were very particular 'other' circumstances, so that was not, would never be, an option. Had the 'culprit' not been formally identified and even tried and found guilty (albeit ironically with a huge dose of 'understanding' on the part of the court and the judge in particular) then possibly - probably even - perhaps James might have been tempted to compromise and make excuses. Who can say what a dire situation can make any one of us overlook. James could have chosen to believe that he was mistaken about the fate of his wife and that at worst it had been some kind of freak accident. That they were covering up some kind of failing rather than an actual crime. That he had misread the signs. It would have been so much easier to have not known, not blamed, not shunned the very people who could make his life 100% easier now. But James was not so easily wooed or so selfish and self-obsessed that his conscience could ever contemplate such a thing. So he did not have the company of his family. But then for the time being, neither did Helen. Though this presented the father with a very practical dilemma, it was psychologically at least a temporary safeguard for the daughter.

So the routine was set. James and Helen lived - at least slept - on the top floor of a large terraced house, with a good garden for her to play in and with both the other floors full to the brim with hard-working adults and noisy children. Helen would have been described as 'shy' by those adults, and 'strange' by those children, though a psychiatrist would have written down 'introvert, impassive, detached' - possibly even 'damaged'. Probably not, what they may have really felt, - since how inhumane to label one so young - 'dangerous' - a time-bomb waiting to explode. But it was just after a major war. Lots of people, not least those returning from the fighting, or those recovering from major trauma - and in some cases traumas, since they had returned from hell to find tragedy - were 'damaged' to some extent. There was never any reason, and certainly no opportunity, to 'refer' such a child for specialist assessment, let alone help. She was just labelled as 'quiet', 'moody', 'shy', 'odd', 'secretive' - depending upon the nature and source of the description.

So for a number of years, Helen spent her time between 'home' and Auntie Maeve's house, attending school with the others, and sleeping over, or returning home, depending upon her father's shifts or social activities. She seemed 'resigned' rather than 'at home' in either place, though remained an enigma even to Maeve, who probably knew her better than most, though she would later say that she never really understood her at all. Kevin was the person, given a choice, that she gravitated towards the most if he was not working.

She was outwardly friendly and totally obedient around Maeve - "too good and somehow watchful and suspicious" was how it seemed to this surrogate mother, who was more used to the healthy 'naughtiness' of her own brood. Despite the reluctance of her earliest years, as she grew, Helen seemed to take to men better than women, to the boys in the family more than the girls. She was not hostile or aggressive, but was definitely more relaxed when in male company. They put it down to only having a male figure at home, and no mother to relate to from her early years.

Eventually, as was only to be expected, James found himself a new love. James had never reneged on the promises that he made when he converted to the Catholic faith, and attended Mass every Sunday, usually for the early service which was designed especially to take into consideration some of the younger children. Maeve was usually there with her clan, though Kevin was less diligent, and sometimes genuinely could not attend with the family because he worked as a ganger on the railways, and sometimes had to - or chose to - work and earn a bit of overtime.

Maeve had been on the look-out for a 'suitable' new romance for James for quite a long time. She had become aware of a new face in the neighbourhood, and became even more interested when that face was seen for a few Sundays at Mass. She monitored the situation for several months until deciding that such a circumstance could not be allowed to pass her by. It did not take Maeve long to engineer an opportunity to strike up an acquaintance with this young woman. She was probably mid-twenties, Maeve guessed likely to be European - Spanish perhaps or Italian. She was staying with the Manzini's who ran the local deli, so more likely Italian, she thought.

It turned out that the young woman's name was Sofia Tadei and she had been born in Scotland, but her parents were originally from Bari in Southern Italy. She had been living in Edinburgh and had trained as a nurse up there. Her parents had decided to return to Italy when her grandfather died, and the family's olive grove and small holding became too much for her grandmother to manage alone.

Sofia preferred to remain in the UK. Though she was already well into her twenties, in order to make her father feel more comfortable about leaving her behind, she had, agreed to move to London in order to be closer, at least temporarily, to her father's sister, her aunt, Magdalena Manzini. She had been secretly delighted to have this new independence, and was even more content to secure a long-cherished job as a paediatric nurse in the neonatal unit of the Middlesex Hospital. In Maeve's view, if she had drawn up a shopping list for the ideal candidate, Sofia would have ticked all the boxes! She was ideal!

Maeve was delighted and set about 'match-making' straight away, much to the amusement of Kevin, who pretended, in order to get a rise out of her, to fancy Sofia himself. Maeve laughed this off, and said she'd pack his bag for him if he wanted to try his luck - she was in the mood for a change herself, as it happened. Both of them knew that no such change would ever take place, since they were absolutely content with one another, and neither had any need or desire to alter their lot in life. James was very envious of their happiness, and was easily persuaded by Maeve's match-making.

So the whole plan went surprisingly smoothly and Sofia was as smitten with James as he was with her. After what seemed like a very short courtship, much to the mixed feelings of Sophie's aunt and uncle, who were glad to hand over the responsibility, though somewhat scared to bring down the wrath of her parents if they thought it was all a bit rushed. The couple did not bother with any kind of engagement, and following a quiet wedding attended just by close friends and Sofia's family, they settled down to married life.

Sofia continued to work at the hospital, and proved a thoroughly efficient, caring and easy to live with wife, who attempted to offer the same attributes to her step-daughter with limited success.

Though she went out of her way to get on with Helen, it was always an uphill battle. Sofia's profession must have accustomed her to stress and to dealing with recalcitrant people, with difficult events and unsettling outcomes, but that could not protect her from the silent, aloof and mistrustful young person waiting and watching in what was, after all her own home too. It certainly did not mean that Sofia was in any way prepared for the rocky road ahead.

Over the next few years, Helen had spent probably more of her time with Maeve and Kevin than she had at home, but no real 'rows' had occurred - not even the tantrums that one might have anticipated with normal young person accepting a stepmother and approaching puberty and adulthood. Sofia and James had still produced no children of their own, no brothers or sisters for Helen. Maeve sometimes joked secretly with Kevin that Sofia must have been put off the whole idea of motherhood by living with the stepchild from the dark side! Though Helen was always polite to Sofia, she was always detached, watchful, accepting but certainly not affectionate.

In reality, though, Sofia's failure to fall pregnant was solely the fault of mother-nature herself, and was very much a sadness for both her and James. Anyway, for whatever reason within the first few years of marriage, no babies had been conceived.

To everybody's relief, mother-nature finally relented and when Helen was a couple of months past her 14th birthday, two things happened in relatively quick succession which had a profound effect on Helen. One for the better. One decidedly for the worst. Sofia found that after many barren years, she was finally pregnant. James was delighted, and Sofia was beside herself with excitement and relief. In those days prior to the possibility of IVF treatment, it was in the lap of the gods whether one was given the blessing of a family or not. Despite that, as a reward for patience and long-suffering, Sofia found that she was not just pregnant, but pregnant with twins. It had been thought - and voiced - by many that Helen would take this badly, being already of a taciturn temperament and having been the only apple in the barrel for her entire life. Sofia in particular was concerned, not so much that the new arrivals would upset her relationship with her step-daughter, since the two were at best polite strangers sharing a house anyway, but that it would cause friction for them all. Knowing how delighted James was, he was bound to lavish his new infants with bottomless love, gifts and time. It was in his nature, and she knew that he had been awaiting this event for a very long time. He would not mean to side-line Helen, but her disconcerting inability to reciprocate any sign of affection and her almost eerie aura of detachment made it very difficult for a tactile person to persevere. James would not mean to transfer his affections, but he probably would seem to do so.

Helen's school had many times raised the suggestion that they might organise some kind of psychiatric assessment for her, but James had been not only reluctant, but downright offended, to even discuss let alone accept this offer. So she was quiet and shy. She was very much a loner. But so what? Was that a sin? Did every child have to be the life and soul of the party? He clung to the fact - which was probably sound to some extent - that she was perfectly at home with Maeve's clan, so could not be as 'introverted' and 'withdrawn' as all that. There were probably just no children in her class she felt any kind of pull towards! She was a bright girl, so they were probably too babyish for her! The school reassured James that they were only suggesting she might need a bit of support, because to lose her mother under such appalling circumstances would have an effect on any child, and it was prudent to be far-sighted and organise some kind of 'intervention' if it would help her 'come to terms' with her loss. James had already been disconcerted to realise that the school knew how Elizabeth had died, but was completely mortified that they knew all of the facts! To think that they must also know that it was a relative of his that had been sent to jail for it was a terrible blow. It was not often that James got angry or visibly upset, but his sheer embarrassment made him react aggressively, which only increased the school's concern over the withdrawn and friendless girl who attended school regularly, worked at her lessons well, but made no attempt to integrate with her classmates, or show anything other than polite indifference towards the staff. Usually young people had at least one teacher that they felt 'comfortable' with, who they related to and felt able to approach. Helen had no such confidante. She just seemed isolated and insular - totally controlled and self-possessed. She did not seem to feel any lack, but the school found her demeanour unusual and alien.

The Headmistress had become anxious to be seen to be doing something, when Helen's Form Mistress had expressed the view, in a staff meeting, that she had been reading a medical journal and was concerned that Helen showed signs of what that publication had referred to as something called 'autism'. It was a diagnosis which was still in its infancy, she said, and studies were on-going, but it appeared to affect young people and from what she read, some of the symptoms were certainly recognisable in Helen Collier.

Had anybody asked Maeve, she would have been able to reassure them that Helen was not always quiet and withdrawn. She was perfectly able to get along with others and participate. Around her house, and particularly around Kevin, she had got quite used to competing for attention with the others. It was true that she was certainly quieter than her own kids, but not noticeably withdrawn or isolated. She had taken her place within the family, competing with the other children for Maeve's attention, and even more so, Kevin's. But Maeve had her own concerns, different from the school, but just as worrying. She knew that Helen had an awful lot of 'adult' thoughts locked up in her young head, she had much more going on in her brain than many - indeed probably all - of Maeve's kids put together. Helen had memories and insights that had caused her to have nightmares and panic attacks ever since she was very little. James had been paternal and caring, but had very much smothered these and rationalised them: she was tired, she ate too late, she had been read a scary story, one of the children had upset her. He had never allowed - let alone encouraged - her to face her demons and have them dealt with. He was not a bad or unintelligent father, he genuinely thought that her fears and worries were just the normal 'bogeyman' or 'ghostie' fears that all children have.

When Sofia was 7 months pregnant, the doctors began deliberating how much longer she could be left before trying to induce the confinement. Helen was revising for her mock General Certificate exams and in a relatively sanguine state of mind. From the very beginning she had taken the news of the babies very well, and had been more animated about her new brothers or sisters than she had been about anything previously. She did not seem resentful or jealous at all, and had even been affectionate and helpful to Sofia when the weight of the twins was making normal chores more difficult and more tiring. She had spoken often about being glad that her father - and of course Sofia - would have children in their lives when she was no longer around. Sofia and James naturally assumed that she meant when she was living her own life, finding her own way in the world.

They hoped she would go to university, or as Sofia sometimes suggested, nurse training. Maeve, who got drawn into such discussions, was not at all sure that the caring professions were quite right for Helen. She had many attributes, but she definitely did not seem like a 'people person'! Though James was proud as punch, as always he still felt somewhat distanced from his daughter. She was in absolutely no way like her mother, she was in no way like himself. She now *looked* a bit like Elizabeth, but the silent, distant, self-contained young women was a stranger to him, and always had been.

The norm in James's own family had been to not take schooling or academic achievement very seriously. Life had mostly dictated that men went out and earned money as soon as they could, and girls settled down, married and had babies - not always in that order - as early as they could. He had, though, learned a lot from both his wives, and he saw no reason why he should not expect more for his daughter.

At almost eight months into her pregnancy, the hospital decided it was time to deliver Sofia's heavy load. The birth went very well, and everybody was very relieved. God - being very kind to Sofia after her long wait - provided both a boy and a girl. The family complete. The little boy was named Charles. That obviously became Charlie to his father, Charles to his mother, and Carlo to Sofia's doting aunt and uncle. Her parents too when they wrote pleaded for photographs, and bemoaned the fact that they lived so far away. The tiny girl was named Angelina; Angel to her father - both in name and description.

Helen proved a model step-daughter and big sister, and James was relieved and definitely impressed by his caring and helpful daughter. He was positively crowing and had absolutely no wish for her to be any other way. He chuckled to himself to remember the school telling him that she was not right! He had no idea what 'autism' was but it sounded like some kind of mental problem. They should see her now! No, he would not have her any other way. She was just perfect: Not at all like the children of all his work colleagues - including Kevin - who were forever moaning and groaning and permanently perplexed by this new breed of creature that inhabited their homes! These 'teenagers' as the papers seemed to refer to them nowadays were absolutely nothing like youngsters 'in their day'! In 'their day' you were either a child or an adult - there was no special status given or expected just because you had an 'een' at the end of your age. Most of the men doing the complaining had been sent out to work at 14, and had neither time nor money to go cavorting around gyrating to this 'bloody rock and roll rubbish' or spending a fortune on outlandish clothes and swooning at these so called 'heart throbs'.

So all was perfect within the Collier household. They apparently all lived quite harmoniously and felt sorry for the rest of the world. It was testimony to the forbearance of them all that it worked at all. Actual space was at a premium. Though the babies, at least for the first several months were sleeping in their parents' room, the accommodation only really had one proper bedroom. The plan was - although Sofia was careful never ever to voice it - that when Helen left for university, the twins would move into her space. For the time being, though, Helen remained in the curtained off portion of the main living area, but was now surrounded by a good deal of the twins' paraphernalia, since there was no other place to put it. Helen had occupied and kept this little corner of their world pristine and immaculate for many years, ever since she was old enough not to be sleeping in a small cot bed in her father's room, and long before he shared his life with Sofia, and even longer before they were in turn joined by Charlie and Angelina. If she found this new clutter and intrusion into her little bit of peace and quiet irksome and unfair, she certainly did not express this view. To somebody like Maeve, who probably knew her better than anybody, having virtually witnessed her birth, but without the bias of being actual 'family', there was something disconcerting about it all. The girl was too controlled, too polite, too accommodating.

The family were finally on the Council housing list, and it was hoped that they could be rehoused now with two new family members, one male, one female. They were existing effectively in the same accommodation that Maeve had found for James all those years ago, one floor of a multi-occupancy house. Not the worse conditions they knew - many others were worse off - but Council housing stock had blossomed due to the rebuilding programmes necessary after the war. Given their situation there was every hope that they could get a house, or at least a purpose-built flat or maisonette quite quickly. They had applied very late to the Council for rehousing because neither James nor Sofia had wanted to accept their reliance on such a move. They had hoped to remain in independent rented housing - obviously not able to even contemplate buying a place of their own - but with their reduced circumstances without Sofia's wage coming in, and the expense of the twins, they had no option but to accept their situation. The offer that they received when the twins were eight months was disappointing. It would have meant them moving right away from anything and anybody they knew. James would have had to find another job, and Helen would have had to change school - at a very important time, the lead up year to her General Certificate. None of that seemed fair to Sofia so she insisted that they decline the offer and hope for another.

The second important event was less welcome. When the twins were approaching their first birthday, James came home from work one day, not at all his usual cheerful and considerate self. He seemed unusually withdrawn and engrossed in his own thoughts, even paying only superficial attention to his baby son and daughter.

Helen was also home. She had seemed much more integrated into the family since the arrival of the twins, and was helpful, though still not particularly talkative or overtly affectionate towards Sofia - not hostile, just not daughterly. She had spent less time at Maeve's home over the past few months as well, though Maeve was a frequent visitor to their home now, assisting the new mother and 'keeping her hand in'. Her own youngest was now no longer a baby and she missed the excitement and even the drudgery. Though she and Kevin had made no decision to stop their family at 7 children (now ranging between 18 and 5) it seemed that nature had taken a hand and decided that enough was enough anyway.

After the twins had been put down to sleep, at least temporarily, because though Sofia, with Maeve's advice and experience, had got the twins into a good routine, and they had been eating well and sleeping well, their good sleeping pattern had latterly been thrown into disarray because they were both teething badly. When one woke, it disturbed the other one, and so nights were somewhat chaotic. James was talking quietly to Sofia in the cluttered but homely kitchen cum living room; Helen was sitting on her bed ostensibly reading.

Realising James's strange and thoughtful mood, which was very unlike him, Sofia was sitting pretending to sew, with quite a lot of trepidation. She did not know why she should feel fearful or anxious, but she had never known her husband in this kind of mood before. James had never talked very much about Elizabeth and the events of the past, but obviously Sofia was aware of what had happened, not least because her aunt and uncle had lived locally for many years and it had been the talk of the neighbourhood when it was all 'going on'. She never spoke about it, and was careful not to do or say anything that reminded James, or Helen. She was then both relieved and surprised when he suddenly said "Guess who I saw today?" He was trying to speak in a low muffled voice so as not to peek his daughter's interest. "Beatrice - you know, my niece - the one who …. she must have been released. The years seem to have flown!"

Obviously since her 'door' was a mere curtain, it did not take long for James's hushed tones to peak his daughter's curiosity and she found it impossible not to listen. She was silent as a mouse, and though she had not originally intended to eavesdrop their conversation, she caught the name 'Beatrice' and could not then carry on reading her book, as though she had heard nothing.

"Did you speak to her?" said Sofia.

"Course not! What would I say. I'd sooner spit in her eye!"

They had not heard Helen move and so were unaware that she was standing as close as she dared, in the shadows, trying to listen but not to be seen.

"Where was she?"

"Walking along the High Street, bold as brass, not a care in the world!"

"Must be living back around here again, do you think?"

"Back in Percival Street, I guess. Logical, I suppose."

"I thought your mother died? Who is living there now?"

"Yes - three years ago. I only know cos a mate of mine who used to be on the dust told me - he had heard from my brother-in-law in the pub. My sister is there now - she was living there anyway - and I guess all the children - probably not children now, unless its children of children! Nothing would surprise me!"

Helen returned to her nook, but no longer engrossed herself in her reading. She had more to think about now. She had been waiting for this for a very long time. In some ways, she considered that her whole life - her full 15 years - had been leading up to this moment.

Having sat very quietly for the best part of half an hour, still lost in thought, she mechanically got into her pyjamas, went downstairs to the shared bathroom, used the toilet, cleaned her teeth, and returned to her alcove. She got her uniform and bag ready for the morning, as she did every week-night before going into the kitchen to get herself a drink and say goodnight to her father and Sofia, just like it was a normal night! Which it certainly was not! 'Normal' would not be a word that would ever be used again with regard to Helen as a result of that conversation.

Chapter 11: Renewing acquaintances

The day began as normal. Helen was up very early and cheerfully helped with the twins. James had long since left for work - now on the railways, a ganger working on the track with Kevin. Sofia was usually surprisingly intuitive of Helen's moods and deeper thoughts, given the fact that there was no blood tie whatsoever between them, but her twins had become her world and most other things had become secondary. She was finding looking after her own two babies far more difficult than she had ever thought, and realised now, as a nurse, how often she had side-lined the poor parents and only paid lip-service to their trauma and worry. She was finding motherhood exhausting - far more exhausting than the drama on the neonatal intensive care ward and she was annoyed and upset with herself for not being able to be the perfect, the unflappable, the super-efficient mother who never panicked, never got flustered and always knew what to do, and when to do it. It was not the same, she found, taking responsibility for your own precious little lives. So she was glad of Helen's help, and acknowledged that on many occasions she would not have been able to cope without it.

Helen eventually left for school, setting off at the normal time, dressed in uniform, set for the day. She attended the Convent

School, a journey of seven or eight stops on the underground. However, on this particular morning, she went off in a completely different direction and having caught a bus took the very short journey in the direction of what she had long since identified as her grandmother's house. She had read plenty reports in the newspapers over the years and had made it her business to pump anybody she could, seek out what information she could, and prepare for this time.

From the bits of the conversation that she had listened into the previous night, she now knew that the family were - or some of them were - still living at the same address. It was at least a place to start. When the bus arrived at the closest stop, she was suddenly at a loss to know exactly what to do. She was hoping that, since she had set off very early, if she was lucky, she might be able to catch somebody, or some bodies, leaving for school, for work, for somewhere. She needed to be able to put names to faces, and faces to places. She considered them all guilty, but acknowledged that some were more guilty than others. She would have to weigh up the various options. She would be judge and jury - maybe even executioner. She found the whole prospect not at all daunting or scary - it was just inevitable. She considered that the payment that had thus far been paid was completely inadequate for the crime committed, and she needed to redress the balance. The law had had their chance, and they had reneged on it. 15 years - which had obviously not even been that - for a life was just not enough. Beatrice's daughter - who must be now about 13 or so - had her mother back, whereas she, Helen, would never get her mother back. She was not unhappy with Sofia - she was certainly not the evil stepmother - but that was not the point. The only fact was that Beatrice - her cousin - a much older cousin, obviously, but a cousin nonetheless - had robbed her of her mother. She had taken away something that could not be replaced. No amount of years in prison could make it right, but it had been such a little time - hardly anything at all. People got more for burglary or bank robbing! They were saying that her mother's life was not worth more than 'things' - money, jewellery, tellies, cars!

Helen had not really planned this part of the mission - she had pictured the outcome many times, but the getting there had not formed part of her imaginings. She was standing on the corner of Percival Street and the High Street, sheltering in the doorway of a public house, which at that time in the morning was closed and locked up. The publican, after a very late night - or perhaps really early morning - was still fast asleep in bed and there were no lights visible on any of the floors. She still looked very conspicuous standing there in her brown school uniform, lisle stockings and boater hat. Worse still, in order to keep up the charade for Sofia that she was off to school as usual, that being a Wednesday, she also had a violin in a case together with her satchel on her back. More than one bright spark going past asked her to 'play us a tune then, love', whilst others recognising the convent school uniform went one better and said 'let's 'ave an 'ymm then, ducks'! Helen was not one to be bothered in any way with such embarrassments. She had had a lifetime - a relatively short lifetime, of course, but a lifetime just the same - of protecting herself from all the comments, the head-shaking, the pity of adults, and the barbs, the name-calling and the cruelty of children, not to mention the mickey-taking of the teenagers when her 'story' had been spread around the schools and the neighbourhoods. Maeve, Kevin and their brood had not only protected her but had taught and prepared her well, and with their nurturing and what could only have been an inherited trait from both sides of her gene pool, she had built a cast-iron shell. She had become a firm believer in the fact that it is impossible to bully somebody who cannot and will not be bullied, and it is impossible to hurt somebody who is numb and oblivious to all hurts.

After about twenty minutes, and just as it started to rain quite heavily, the door of 7 Percival Street opened and two people came out - a young girl and an older woman. The woman tried to put her arm around the girl's shoulders, and was digging into her purse for some money, but though the girl seemed happy enough to accept the money - and what young person would not - she was having none of the hugs or familiarity that was on offer from the woman. This was a stroke of luck - better than Helen could have expected so early on - because, having been to the library and researched the background to her mother's murder, and even vaguely remembering bits and pieces of her babyhood, she recognised Beatrice, and made the assumption that this must be her daughter, who, she had read, was called Susan.

The girl looked embarrassed at her mother's efforts at closeness and seemed eager to make her own way off to school without the chaperone. Eventually she gave up on subtleties, and shrugged off her mother's arm and ran as fast as she could, leaving the woman standing forlorn on the opposite corner to where Helen was watching intently.

Having made the first 'sighting' Helen then took herself off to school, excusing her lateness by laying the blame on her new twin step-siblings. Mother Annunciata, the nun on 'Portress's Duty' - or in reality the gate-keeper *(though that would have been a far too ungenteel (albeit accurate!) a description for the nuns)* - was suitably impressed that Helen had been so helpful and understood completely that life was not quite going as smoothly in the Collier household as it once had been - and for a wonderful and miraculous reason - God's gift of two bonny, healthy and holy babies. May God bless them all! Helen took herself off to class. A Latin lesson, an opportunity to concentrate not on declension but on intention.

The Latin teacher, a lay teacher, Miss Knight must have arrived at her first teaching post, delighted to have landed a job at a girls only convent Grammar school where the pupils were bound to be not only intelligent but well-mannered and friendly. How was she to know the fallacy of such an assumption! Her own convent boarding school education had been in a quiet and peaceful rural idyll in the wilds of Devon, where the loudest noises were the baaing of sheep or bird song at dawn. All this, a far cry from a day school - convent or otherwise - in the very heart of the metropolis. Where she found herself now was an animal of quite a different nature! This was a school - an urban school in the very heart of a wide awake metropolis. Not the hunting, shooting fishing, rural backwater this - more a kind of city wild west, where the pupils of any school - even a convent grammar school - had found it necessary to be street wise in order to survive in the surrounding environment of both their homes and their school. Chapel during the day, maybe, but after they walked out of the door, they needed all their wits about them! It was a question of self-preservation. Naturally some of this edge could not be left at the school door, and not infrequently spilled over into the school yard, or the classroom. The girls were definitely not crocheting pot-holders like the girls in Miss Knight's previous location, and though there were undoubtedly far worse schools, with far worse pupils, these ones were certainly bad enough for this poor first timer, and decidedly a far cry from what the poor woman had been anticipating.

Miss Knight's lesson was usually good value for 'doing one's own thing'. She could be brought to tears very easily and only too readily gave up on any attempt at actual teaching. To impart any kind of deeper knowledge at a level beyond rote, would have necessitated some method of controlling or disciplining her pupils. She almost always took the easy option; merely instructing people 'to read and translate' random passages or chapters. She had not, since mid-way through lesson one, day one, ever again dared to run the gauntlet of trying to teach the brightest young things of the Upper Fifth to prepare for their GCE Latin exam. In her defence, most of them would have preferred to have been allowed to go off school premises to do 'cookery' or 'domestic science', but these girls, unfortunately for Miss Knight, were deemed to be 'too bright' for such a parochial curriculum. That fact made it doubly bad news for their misfortunate teacher since their supposedly superior brain-cells made them also ever more devious at devising ways to plague and torment her.

Helen, however, was not one of the more disruptive members of the set. She was considered aloof and 'odd' by her form members, though she also gave off a kind of 'hands off' aura which prevented her from being bullied. The other girls were surprisingly careful around her - a kind of respect springing from a wariness and knowledge that 'still waters ran deep' and that there was much more to her than met the eye. Many of them formed cliques, and these cliques led a kind of hierarchical existence, but with the ever fluctuating levels of growth spurt, maturity and 'experience of the outside world', i.e. boyfriends, sexual adventures, etc., no group permanently dominated by divine right, which made for a more volatile, but less 'bullying' atmosphere. No group dared really 'bully' today, because who knew what tomorrow might bring! However, Helen, a friend to none, but also an enemy to none, lived in middle earth, somewhere betwixt and between the factions, never part of them, never trusted by them, but somehow respected by them. Individually they were fearful, collectively they were intrigued and wary.

So on the day of her first sighting of her 'cousin' Beatrice, her mother's murderer, Helen chose to sit towards the back of the classroom, way over near the window where she was at liberty to consider her actions, and her future - short though it might be. She had been more affected than she thought she would be by coming almost face to face with Beatrice's daughter (whom she had learned from the newspaper reports over the years was called Susan). She realised that she too, in a way, had been 'motherless' for all, or certainly most, of her growing up years. She had not thought that she would feel any kind of kinship or, for heaven's sake, sympathy, with any of them, but her mind careered about without her permission. It veered between empathy and anger. Susan had done nothing personally; Susan's 'loss', though, was not permanent; it was capable of being put right - as now it had been – albeit many years on. Her own 'loss' was permanent. Then too, Susan's loss had been brought about by her mother's actions - not hers specifically, it had to be said - but it was them! That family! (*It made it worse if she took that thought further and dwelt on the fact that it was her family too, so she tried never to do so. Somehow her father's alienation from them meant that she could push the connection to the back of her mind and not be reminded of the closeness. Not be reminded of the fact that, judging from the newspaper articles, and listening to the stories told by Maeve, the mastermind of everything that went on in that household was her own grandmother!)* Her own loss was not only permanent, but both she and her poor murdered mother were innocent victims in all this! Her cousin certainly could not say that! Ultimately, Helen's hatred and need for revenge far outweighed any fellow-feeling she might temporarily feel towards Susan. Omelettes and eggs, eggs and omelettes!

Susan would get over it, the same as her father would get over her. He had the twins now. That was a relief. Her only concern now was whether it was possible to force herself to wait it out until she was officially 'an adult'. The last thing she wanted was to be treated as a naughty child and sent to a remand home, or a borstal or something. She was not sure how quickly one became liable for capital punishment, but hoped it was 16. She would have to check. After all she could marry at 16? So in 6 months' time would she or would she not be adult enough to hang? That was something she would have to investigate. Carefully! Not the sort of thing you could easily ask a teacher, or worse still a parent? It would have to be couched in an academic kind of way …. not easy, especially with her background and unfortunate history.

Chapter 12:   Fraternising with the enemy

Having continued her 'research', Helen waited the necessary few months until she had well and truly turned 16 so as to leave no margin for error.   She made one last reconnoitre of Percival Street to check that those who she thought lived there, were still in residence.   Then, the following Friday, she casually informed Sofia on leaving for school that it was a school 'feast day' and they had been told that for a payment of 2 shillings and 6 pence into the Missions Box, they could wear their own clothes.   They could go to school in mufti just so long as their idea of mufti was not trousers, or mini-skirts or anything too flashy or inappropriate.   Sofia had no reason to doubt this statement.

Helen's lie was almost put to the test because for once she had misjudged the reaction of her stepmother, who on contemplating this injustice became appalled that the nuns were asking for such a large sum from school girls!   Sofia was at the best of times not a massive fan of nuns.   She had not fared well at school with nuns, not least because her father was a well-known Communist and they considered him, therefore, not that much different from Old Nick himself!   Despite the fact that her father had never stopped her mother attending Mass or bringing his daughter up as a good

Catholic girl, they had never let Sofia forget the fact that she was living with Satan - or at least his representative here on earth. They often publicly called upon the other girls to pray at Assembly for 'heathens' and 'atheists' and that God might give their families the strength to withstand the terrible influences within their homes. Not being stupid, and to a large extent also fearing that the 'heathen' might make a personal intervention and bring his own wrath down upon them regardless of any divine protection, they never actually uttered her name - though they looked at her pityingly, and nodded in her direction with a show of sympathy and understanding that even the most insensitive onlooker would have difficulty misreading! Despite that, she had grown into a clean living and comparatively devout woman, but one with a healthy and well-reasoned mistrust and dislike of nuns. She hid this from nobody. She gave her honest opinion about them, as they had about her father and her family. Most - though even she acknowledged not all - of them were petty dictators and mean-spirited women. They gave nothing to the world. They hid behind the cloister pretending to do so for the best of intentions, when most of them were there because it provided an alternative to facing reality. It saved them from any responsibility for providing for themselves, let alone a family. They were protected from life and need and anybody's dependency; it provided a roof, food, companionship, and a feeling of superiority, without having to earn a proper living in the harsh and competitive world outside the privileged and sanitised world of the cloister. There would never be any need to meet eyeball to eyeball the sins, temptations and practical challenges that those they so frequently criticised must face! Oh yes, she could wax lyrical and had she still had the time, energy and was she not hampered by 12 feeds a day, and 12 lots of nappy changing, let alone the copper permanently boiling with washing, she would have gone to that convent and given them a piece of her mind. Asking school children to pay that kind of money showed just how money-grabbing they were. Missions indeed - another cake each for tea, more likely!

Helen had to quickly backtrack and reassure her that it was not a 'compulsory' levy and they could give as little as they liked - or nothing even - but just not *more than* 2s6d. Some of the girls said the price of going to the pictures was about that, which was how Mother Patricia had landed on that amount - but as the maximum, definitely not the amount they had to pay … it was absolutely not a …. it was voluntary - not a demand - they could still wear their own clothes, whether they paid or not …. it was just a suggestion! Helen's attempts were getting more and more frenzied as she tried to extricate herself from her own lie!

Sofia was only partially mollified and had she the time and if she was once again a free agent, she would have not been so easily fobbed off.

Helen was sorry she had mentioned the money. She only threw that in when Sofia noticed that she was taking money from her savings jar. Sofia knew that Helen had been saving up for a box brownie camera and was sad that she was having to dip into it. She would have willingly given Helen a shilling or two rather than see her raid her own hard-won savings, but now that she was not working and only one wage was coming into the house, money was not all that plentiful. In every way Helen's unfortunate decision to over-elaborate about the 'levy' by the nuns was a major mistake. It was a wonder that she managed to leave the house, with her money, in her 'day clothes' without Sofia insisting on putting the babies in their pram and stalking off to vent her spleen on Mother Patricia and her entourage! Oh what a tangled web we weave, when first we practice to deceive!

So Helen made a very quick exit and just had to hope that the babies kept Sofia sufficiently busy all day to prevent her from thinking too deeply about the whole story. Her luck - or not, depending upon one's point of view - was in, because before the hour was passed, Sofia was up to her neck in crying babies, potato peelings, hissing copper boilers and a mountain of dirty terry towelling nappies and pram sheets.

Chapter 13: To stalk or confront?

Helen set off, catching the bus once again, timing her arrival to match the previous recces when she frequently had watched her cousins leave the house. She was hoping, since it was another school day, that the pattern would be the same, and that it was just the normal routine for a week-day.

She only had to wait for about fifteen minutes when, on cue, the person that she had recognised as Beatrice Collier left the house, together with the younger girl. Though no photographs had appeared in the cuttings of Beatrice's little daughter, who was a mere baby when she was charged, arrested and sentenced, Helen had decided to 'assume' that this young girl was the daughter, Susan.

The papers had said that Beatrice had been about 6 months pregnant when she had murdered her mother - indeed the Defence, and the papers, had made a big thing of that, as though that was an excuse for everything! Did that mean that every pregnant woman could be excused for going around and murdering people! Helen thought not! What kind of excuse was that! If all the pregnant women went around murdering people because they were 'in a delicate condition (to paraphrase the newspapers!) then nobody would be safe, given the birth-rate - every second woman was pregnant, especially in the aftermath of the war! So .... anyway, back to her more immediate thoughts! If Helen had been, say, two when her mother was killed, that would mean, then that .... Yes, if she was now 16, then Susan must be about 13 or 14 even.

Justice had not been served up to now. Susan would get over it - after all what you've never had, you don't really miss, do you? Beatrice had been in prison for almost all of the girl's life anyway, hadn't she?

This time, a decision had to be made. Did she follow the woman or the girl? There was a risk in getting to know the girl - would she then be strong enough to cause her pain? Helen had had a long time to dwell on her own feelings - her own capabilities, and was sure - well fairly sure - that she would follow through, regardless.
She did think, therefore, that she would quite like to get some kind of insight into her - what was she? - her second cousin? - first cousin once removed? It always seems so complicated to work it out - anyway, into the girl's life. What was she like? Was she nice or nasty? A bully - that would make it easier, or just an ordinary girl. The daughter of a murderer? That did not make her a bully, no more

than Helen being the daughter of a murdered woman made her a victim! A victim she was not; a victim she would never be. She may die a non-natural death, but it would be one she would choose, and one that she would bring upon herself. No, she was not, would never be, a victim! Her future, her end, was of her own choosing, her own design, almost.

So, she set off closely following her quarry until they separated at the tube station entrance, when Beatrice went off towards the bus, and Susan made her way towards the ticket office to pay for her journey. This was a bit of a nuisance for Helen because she had to move quite swiftly, getting closer to Susan than she would have liked at this juncture, in order to hear where she needed to buy a ticket to. As luck would have it, the girl did not seem to notice her, and they both bought their train tickets, and made their way towards the escalator.

Helen had become a bit of a wanderer over the years, finding it very easy to avoid being in any given place at any given time. When she was not at home with her father and Sofia, they assumed that she was at Maeve's, and Maeve assumed that she was at home. She was, therefore, quite comfortable travelling around by herself and as a 15-year-old living in London, she was completely at home on the underground system - 'the tube'. As she followed Susan down the escalator and onto the Southbound platform, she was sharp enough to see an unexpected but very fortuitous event. As Susan pushed her way through a gaggle of young boys who had congregated around the narrow passageway linking the northbound from the southbound tracks, she dropped her purse (*Helen knew this contained her ticket, because she had watched her put it in when she left the payment window*) which she had carelessly shoved into the side pocket of a rucksack she was carrying slung over her shoulder.

Helen could not believe her luck when arriving at that same spot, she saw the purse lying battered from all the clomping boots, but still in situ. She retrieved this gratefully and putting it into her pocket, made a beeline for the train in hot pursuit of Susan.

Most of the tube travellers at that time in the morning were travelling southbound, whereas Susan's school - and apparently that of the boys - was away from the heart of the city, rather than within its heaving and throbbing centre. So she located the girl without too much difficulty, the bulk of the other travellers being the raucous but good natured youths - yobs Sofia would probably have called them - and just a smattering of suited and booted professionals on their way to their places of work in the more leafy and tranquil out of city locations. Susan, Helen discovered, had by then joined two other girls of roughly the same age, and they were chatting together pointedly ignoring the heckling and hectoring of the boys around them who were trying to draw them into conversation. When the next train came in, Helen kept a safe distance, but followed the gaggle through the fast-closing doors and off through the tunnels - the girls and boys to school, Helen to …… she had not the slightest idea!

When the young people all alighted four stops on up the line, Helen's ploy to force an introduction to Susan by 'finding' her purse when the girl was confronted by the ticket collector was somewhat thwarted. At that particular station, the lift up to the outside world was a bit hit or miss. Once again, which apparently was not unusual, all passengers had to climb the 142 stairs which took them up to daylight. The kids seemed unperturbed by this and took it in their stride, but some of the adults - particularly the professional men - complained when they got to the top and asked vociferously just when London Transport were going to do something about the lift situation. It was now not a rare occurrence for paying passengers to have to climb the stairs, but the more normal situation! The young people ignored all of this and jostling and play-fighting the boys left the station, with the far smaller number of girls in the crowd still chatting and laughing as though the lads did not exist. Because of the melee, and the complaining of the grown-ups about the poor service, the ticket collector at the barrier was far too busy fighting his corner on behalf of his employer to check many - indeed any - tickets, and so though Susan fiddled around for her purse in her rucksack, without success, she was, however, able to pass through unembarrassed or unchallenged. Helen could only imagine her discomfiture later when it was time to return home and she had no ticket, no money. *Helen would have been disappointed, because having reported the loss of her purse when she reached school, she was able to 'borrow' her fare home from the School Secretary.*

So Helen followed Susan to her school and had decided that the next day - or whenever she could do so without causing suspicion - she would do the same for her murdering cousin until she knew precisely on a daily basis where people were, and what their routine was about. Planning and precision were the tools she needed. She was not concerned about careful planning so that she could escape detection - 'get away with murder' - literally, since she had no intention of not taking responsibility - indeed credit - for her actions. She did not want the mission to end up a failure - or worse still a fiasco. She wanted to avenge her mother, not make herself look a fool - an eejit as Maeve would say - or be caught before she had succeeded. She would hold onto her cousin's purse which would prove useful to force an introduction at a later date. She might even go knock on the door. She had not really decided whether to 'hide' her identity or announce herself 'loud and proud'. She would see how she felt; how the land lay.

She had the rest of the day to kill - unfortunate phrase, under the circumstances - but she could not return home and could not go to school, so she went to the cinema - a dark and undiscovered place to hide and to think. In those days, the showings of the films were continuous and so it was possible to just sit for as long as she liked for the price of a single entry fee. The main film and the 'B' movie were quite entertaining the first time round, but after that it left a nice long time for her to mull over her best strategy until it was time for her to make an appearance back home again. Susan's purse still nestled inside her bucket bag, which had formed part of her 'mufti' outfit, replacing her satchel. It would have to be returned to its rightful owner - at an appropriate time.

Helen had spent a good part of her young life waiting and brooding. Though she was now feeling relieved that the picture was clearer and it was more of a question of biding her time rather than the indeterminate waiting game it had been in the past, she was not one to rush into anything. It was less that she had any intention of planning her move so that she got away uncaught, unpunished, but she was more concerned that she might give the game away and thus be prevented from succeeding in her mission.

Over the days following her sortie into the world of 'undercover' and 'surveillance' she was quite content to return to normal. She went to school, she acted the dutiful daughter, the helpful big sister. She even turned up once or twice over the next couple of days at Maeve's - a visit she had not made for at least the previous couple of months. She knew this was risky because Helen was well aware that if anybody was going to 'sus' her out and know that there was something going on in her head, it was going to be Maeve. It became almost part of the preparation - on the basis that if she could 'fool' Maeve, then she was safe with everybody. She would have loved to have confided in Maeve, because she valued her clear thinking intelligence more than anybody else. Maeve might appear to all around her to be a laid back, easy going and simple wife and mother, but Helen had long since realised that it was a façade, an act. It was not an act in order to fool anybody or to gain an advantage, it was merely that she was playing the part she had been allocated. If Kevin realised he was married to an intellectually superior being he did not let on, and since he was not an 'omadhaun' either, they were both happy playing the game for the world at large. Most Irish people in those days knew it was safer to appear to be what the world at large believed them to be, the happy, hard-drinking, 'thick Mick' pantomime figures that made them useful as navvies and grafters, entertainers and enablers, offering no challenge to the locals with their higher intellect and more sophisticated manners. Certainly not attempting to compete with them as equals! They were 'safe'. Not 'strange' and 'scary' and 'queer' (in the old fashioned sense!) like 'the Blacks'! No! They looked English, but were not English. By no means as sophisticated and accomplished as the English - indeed a bit thick if the truth be told. But good workers and when they were not drunk or knocking seven bells out of each other, they were pleasant enough. Easy going and generally good company. Always ready to accept themselves as the butt of the joke - indeed laughing along with the rest – without taking offence.

Maeve and Kevin did have more than one late night conversation about Helen and shared their individual concerns about her. She was too 'controlled', too repressed and brooding for their liking - it was not just that she was so different from their own raucous, opinionated, squabbling kids, but she was somehow scarily uptight, and it seemed, watchful, pent up, almost dangerous. They were not fearful for others - they were more fearful for Helen herself. She had always seemed, even as a child, to be completely unconcerned about her own safety - if a child could be described as 'suicidal' there had been times when Maeve had been anxious for Helen's well-being. In the latter years it was as though she was just waiting for something, for what Maeve nor Kevin were completely unable to say, but it was a strange aura to be around. Had she not been a child that they had known and loved - almost as their own - for many years they might have wondered if their own children were safe around her. Not because she would deliberately hurt any of them, but she was so unconcerned about her personal safety that there could be a risk of her leading them into danger. She was not an outgoing girl, not adventurous as such, so it was not so much a physical danger as a kind of carelessness and irrelevance of the implications of any situation that seemed to wave a warning flag.

Over the next few weeks, Helen kept her head down, went to school and displayed no signs of breaking her routine, since this would only have run the risk of opening a dialogue between the nuns and Sofia. She would be silly to make either of these potential obstacles watchful or suspicious. She was more than glad that the time was approaching when she could undertake the role that she had marked out for herself. She had first decided that she was the avenging angel when she was ten or eleven - when she had been old enough to read the newspaper cuttings that she had discovered in a tin box under her father's bed. Old enough to piece this together with pitying looks, the head shaking, the raised eyebrows that tended to accompany her introduction to grown-ups with their embarrassingly over-solicitous attention. That was why she had liked being with Maeve and Kevin and their flock because she had never experienced that 'undercurrent' in their home - if Maeve and even more Kevin had something to say, they had more or less said it. The children had certainly shown her no deference. She had just been one of them - she got no special treatment and no mercy or regard was given just because she 'had a sad start in life'!

It was testament to Helen that in the midst of all this watching and waiting, she managed to sit and complete 10 subjects in her General Certificate of Education. Though there were subjects that she preferred and which came easier to her, she thought she had probably done reasonably well in most of them. It would not matter, of course, since as far as she was concerned such qualifications were going to be an irrelevance. But at least her father and Sofia would have some cause to be proud of her, and, even more importantly, nobody could say that she was in some way 'thick' or not compos mentis enough to understand or take responsibility for her actions. She had no intention of using that kind of 'get out of jail' card.

Chapter 14: The Fateful Day arrives

Helen rose, got washed and dressed, as normal, helped Sofia sit the twins down for their breakfast - more a question of sitting them down to embark upon target practice since they appeared to throw most of their food everywhere except down their own gullets. Helen took time to relish their antics this very special morning, since who knew if, or when, she would be able to relive this normal domestic and familiar scene. In her own head she hoped not - not that she was glad to leave it behind, but it would mean that she had succeeded in her task and the price was now payable. She understood totally the impact, upheaval and sadness that this day would inevitably bring to her family. She had considered in the past that perhaps her plan was cruel in the extreme on her father, since he would have to lose both her mother and herself under the spotlight of public scrutiny. She had been very relieved when he met and married Sofia, and even more so when the twins arrived since they were his family now and he would be able to move on with their help. She had sometimes wished she could let Kevin in on her plans, so that he would be better prepared to help her father at work - his work colleagues were bound to be condemning. She had been sure that Kevin would not understand and would try to thwart her - as any sane man would. She was less sure that he would actually go to the police because she knew that he cared a lot about her and in any case he was not a big fan of the peelers! So it was definitely unlikely - probably impossible. But he would nonetheless try to stop her himself and that would cause even bigger problems. She could do without trying to watch out for him as well. It was too dangerous for him. If he did not manage to prevent her - and she was quite sure he would not be able to - that might lay him open to being thought an accessory before the fact (she had read that in a book when she had been doing her research). It was not a question of after the fact because she was intending to go straight away to the nearest police station and face the music but only once she was quite sure that she had succeeded in her mission. So Kevin of all people needed to be kept completely in the dark.

She left the house now in full school uniform, leaving half an hour early, much to the surprise of Sofia who knew that school days were somewhat more relaxed now that exams had been got out of the way. Helen had told her that she was intending to buy an end of term gift for her form teacher en route. Sofia was suspicious of this tale since it was unlikely that any appropriate shops would be open that early in the morning. She had said nothing about it on Saturday when she would have had more choice. Sofia was sure that the nuns did not smoke, and she hoped the lay teachers also had no such vices. Since at that time in the morning only newsagents and tobacconists were open, it was a poor alibi in all honesty. Sofia smiled to herself thinking that Helen had perhaps got herself a nice young man - which, for a reclusive and introverted young girl would be a step in the right direction. Sofia just hoped she would not get let down and disappointed. She was a sensitive soul and not good with people. She could get quite badly hurt. However, life being hectic and there not being sufficient hours in the day already, Sofia had to leave her stepdaughter's love life to its own devices.

Helen realised that she could have just got rid of Beatrice on the street any time and day, but she had made up her mind that she wanted to make it more meaningful than that. She had been about seven when she had first begun to tap into memories and build up pictures of her past based on her nightmares and her vague recollections. It had not made a lot of sense until she had begun to hear the stories of her mother's death and avidly read and pour over any news or reporting she could lay her hands on which related to it. She suddenly realised that somewhere inside her head she knew that those facts were wrong. Gradually she realised why she knew the facts were wrong. She knew, absolutely and without doubt, that she had been there when her mother was killed - it was not in the open, it was not on a bomb-site, it was within the assumed safety of her grandmother's home. She did not recall all of the detail, but she was absolutely certain about two facts: It was Beatrice and it was in the kitchen of the house in Percival Street. That meant that they had all lied. They had all been party to the cover up, and they had all been responsible for dumping her mother's body - on a bomb-site, like a sack of old rubbish. So it was not sufficient to take Beatrice's life, it was necessary for that to happen within the house - to replicate history. But she would honour Beatrice with more care and respect than they had ever given to her mother. She would not see her lifeless on the street, at the mercy of dogs, rats, voyeurs, the elements. She would not make it necessary for Beatrice's body to lay in a mortuary for months unclaimed, unmourned, unsanctified. She would be the better human being. Acknowledging responsibility immediately so that there was no need to waste time investigating and so that Beatrice could be buried and mourned without too much delay.

Helen had had an ulterior motive the previous week to spend time with Maeve. After Beatrice's trial had finished and the dust had settled, James had been living quietly with Helen trying to keep his head above water and not sink into despair or the bottle. He had his daughter to consider and that was his principal - indeed only - responsibility now. Despite the fact that he was by no means well off, he could not bring himself to sell or profit from the fur coat or the diamond brooch which had largely been responsible for Elizabeth not being quickly buried and forgotten as a derelict or a nobody when she was found. It was the fact that she had the expensive coat and the brooch that had made her a cut above any common or garden corpse that was found and unceremoniously buried in a pauper's grave without investigation or ceremony. He had thought long and hard, and realised her could not bear to have it under his roof, but could not bear to sell it, so he had taken it around to Maeve. Maeve knew only too well that the whole purpose of the gift of the coat by Mrs. Greenberg had been to get Elizabeth, James and baby Helen back on their feet after the war, so she did not feel it was hers to sell or profit from. She did understand, however, that it was hard for James to have it there as a reminder all the time. So she had wrapped it up, put it in an old suitcase with mothballs and put it at the top of her big wardrobe. There it had remained. She had shown it to Helen a few years before when it seemed right that the girl be made aware of facts rather than the fiction and the half-truths that she had been reading about in the old press cuttings. Helen had managed some days previously to struggle the case down from the wardrobe, remove the coat and brooch, and return the case innocently back up as though it had not been disturbed. The coat was bulky and awkward to carry, but she had the presence of mind to bring with her, folded up conveniently small in her voluminous bucket bag, her father's old army kitbag which he had lost track of because she had it hidden away under her bed ever since she had first properly constructed her plan of attack.   She had not known why, but apart from it being a bit of shared history between her father and her mother, she just had an inkling that it might be useful. She stuffed the coat into this, the brooch into her pocket, and managed to get out of the house in the absence of Maeve at the shops, Kevin at work and the rest of the household fighting over whether Connor had cheated at a game of snakes and ladders or not. They hardly knew that she was there, let alone register her departure carrying the very fat kitbag with its contents.

She knew that the fur coat and the brooch were crucial because they linked the two crimes - one past, one to come.   It was difficult, however, to easily work out how it was possible to cart the coat around without it being both cumbersome and conspicuous.   The kitbag made it easier to carry, but was not exactly inconspicuous.
She could hardly wear it without it being even more eye-catching and eyebrow raising.   She had managed to get it home, and hid it in the old chicken house in the back garden.   James had gone through a phase of keeping chickens and bantams, but working long hours and now with Sofia having her hands full with the babies, he had

given them away to the son of one of his workmates who wanted to keep hens and breed rabbits for the table. The hen house was somewhat smelly and cobwebby, but it was more or less dry and unlikely to be visited at least in the short term by any household member.

So leaving the house early, she made her way into the back garden and retrieved the kitbag containing the fur coat. Overnight she had realised that the kitbag and its contents could be all the more useful because they were conspicuous. Particularly with people who cannot help themselves but be inquisitive and on the lookout for a new angle.

The kitbag was definitely cumbersome on public transport, but Helen was not in the frame of mind to be minding about the moans and tuts that she got from people that she bumped into or prevented from getting on because she took up too much room. When she reached her stop, she got off and once again, as she had done on several occasions in rehearsal over the past few months made her way to Percival Street. This time she was sufficiently early that they were unlikely to have left for school or for work. She knew that Beatrice had a job working with one of her mother's old friends who now ran her own hairdressing business. Beatrice was mostly sweeping up and handing rollers and pins to the experienced hairdressers, but she strutted and walked the walk and dressed and preened as though she was the proprietor rather than the gopher. Each time Helen had followed her and watched her antics through the shop window she had had to laugh. The staff - who were probably wary because the owner was obviously a friend of this poser - could often be seen giggling with one another, throwing their eyes to heaven in exasperation or grimacing when her back was turned. Sometimes it was hard for Helen to drag herself away from the pantomime.

Helen on this occasion did not hang about on the corner but walked straight up to the house and knocked on the door. A window opened and a head was thrust out and a voice said "What do you want? We're not buying nothing and …." Helen moved backwards on the pavement so that she could more easily see and be seen by whoever was shouting out of the window.
"No, sorry, I'm not selling anything …. I found something that I think belongs here."

"Oh, well, sorry luv, thought you was a bleedin pedlar or a diddicoy - can't be too careful these days. …. Wait a bit and …… no, on second thoughts, I'm in me scanties here …." With that a key came hurtling out of the window, and the voice said "Let yerself in, ducks, and come up …… I can't hang out of this window any longer I'll get me bleedin' death of cold!"

Well thought Helen, who could have predicted that! There she had been trying to make up her mind what excuse she could give to be invited upstairs when somebody answered the door - she had considered asking to use the toilet, pretending to faint and needing a glass of water, that she was being followed, attacked or molested. ….. all now useless and unnecessary fabrications … and instead here was the key being lobbed out of the window for her use and an unsolicited invitation to come upstairs.

She let herself in. She had wondered, since she was a girl whose head was infinitely more mature than her years would suggest, whether, when push came to shove, she would feel nervous, trepidatious, even guilty. But no. The moment was here - and she felt …. well she felt exhilarated and triumphant. A strange thing was happening too. As she climbed those stairs, she was suddenly transported back to a time, years before and going up and down that same flight on her bottom, scraping the tops of her little stumpy legs and getting splinters in her bum from the bare wood. She recollected, too, at least once being knocked down the bottom few by the on-rushing of the then family dog, Nigger. *(Now of course such a name would be a cause for horror, possibly prosecution even, but then - it seemed to her - it had been quite normal, even affectionate. Different times. Totally different times! The dog was black. He was called Nigger. End of Story.)*

She went up the last few stairs, and found two doors - one to the left, one straight ahead. She had no hesitation - it was now familiar territory. She just knew that the door to the left led into the kitchen, and that in turn led into the front living room, from which Beatrice had thrown the key. She had no idea how her two-year-old head had preserved that information for her 16-year-old legs to act upon, but that was what had happened. She went straight in and not taking time to look round to see if anybody else was in the kitchen, she located the same two people in the room that she had become familiar with. Once she had reached them, in response to a sudden cough in the kitchen, she turned back and saw a figure standing drying cups and hanging them on hooks on a wooden dresser. An older woman. A woman with alarmingly vivid auburn hair hanging lankly down her back, cigarette dangling from a mouth that was short of teeth, which were presumably in a glass somewhere. Far from the face of the woman who had invited her up, this one was scowling, wary looking, annoyed at the intrusion. For a moment even the stoic Helen thought that she had been rumbled, the lack of warmth being so palpable from the direction of this fearsome woman, but still with the cigarette dangling from the mouth, she merely said "You're a bleedin' early visitor, ain't you?   What you got then that's worth being Speedy Gonzales?"

Pulling herself together, and realising that that must be the woman's normal face and manner, she fished around and very carefully retrieved the girls' purse from deep inside the cavernous school bag that she habitually carried about now, which contained everything she did not want Sofia to find at home.
She walked over and handed the purse to the 'mean-faced woman', since she seemed to be the one that was taking charge of the situation.   The woman at the window, still standing in bra and full slip, through which stockings and suspenders were quite visible, but minus anything on her feet or any kind of top clothing.   She was in full view of the window but that did not seem to matter to her at all. She did then, however, walk into the adjoining room and lean over the toothless woman's shoulder to see what was being discussed.

"Oh, bloody 'ell, Susie, it's yours.   That purse you lost - remember - here it is!"

Susan, who had continued to sit on a knobbly looking sofa eating what looked like toast and smelled like Marmite, then had her interest peaked. She got up, still without any real urgency, and came across to inspect the purse.

"Gordon Bennett, Suse, it's still got a ten bob note in it! Well that must be a miracle! Bleedin' hell. Who would have expected that? My faith in the world has been restored, though my respect for people's initiative is a bit dented! Surely this was lost weeks ago. How come it's been sitting around for ages, and still nobody has had the gumption to pocket the dosh. I'm delighted, course I am, but even more I'm bloody amazed."

Susan seemed completely disinterested in where it had been, or how Londoners had suddenly become so honest or lacking in initiative. She took the purse from her mother's hand and said "Thanks!" Just that. No other words. No questions about wheres, whens, hows. Just 'Thanks". She then took the purse out of her mother's hand, gathered up her schoolbag, collected her school blazer which was hanging on a hook just inside the landing door, and left them. Helen heard her heavy school shoes clip clopping down the stairs, and was relieved that she had gone. It was less that she was getting squeamish about doing what she had to do with the girl there - after all she had been there when her mother was murdered - but she did not want to run the risk that with three people there she might be prevented. She did not have any desire to get away with it, but she was not prepared to run the risk of failing. She would do what she had come to do, and then face the consequences.

She was then helped because 'toothless' shrugged, and said "Beattie, you better get moving. You'll be getting the sack, and I ain't going keep you for nothing."
"Right, Mum. Just going". As she said this she started to pull her dress over her head, and Helen knowing that she was never going to have a better opportunity, quickly delved into her voluminous bag and bringing out the long carving knife, quick as a flash darted over and plunged it in up to the hilt into the back of the disadvantaged woman. If Beatrice was surprised, nobody could say, since her head and arms were, at the point of oblivion, still trying to push their way into a very close fitting sheath dress. Appropriately and obligingly bright red. Though that did not prevent the very visible sight of a darker and shinier shade of red which was spreading horribly across the garment and dripping faster and faster onto the floor.

Helen was surprised that the only sound was a kind of gasp - almost a gurgle. Not even enough to make the older woman turn around. Obviously, since she had been addressed as 'Mum', Helen assumed that this must be her aunt, Gladys - or was she her cousin? Helen had always found it difficult to work out the relationships whilst listening to Maeve - never her father - who related the drama, melodrama and sometimes the sheer comedy as relayed by her brilliant mimic of a mother, when she returned from visits. The aunts, cousins, second cousins and first cousins once removed etc. got a bit blurred in the telling, not least because of the disparity in ages between the generations. Her grandmother had her eldest child - a daughter - a good long while before the others, and years before her marriage. That pattern was repeated by the rest, with some/many of them becoming mothers themselves at a very early age too, which further complicated the family tree. Gladys though had featured more prominently in the press coverage, since she took the brunt of the 'blame' for the home and atmosphere that Beatrice had been brought up in which had *'led her to be a depressed and psychiatrically challenged young woman, made worse by her unwanted and unfortunate pregnancy outside of marriage'*, as her Defence Lawyer explained, a fact reinforced by the Judge.

Though Helen had devoured any newspaper cuttings that she could find, the other faces had nonetheless blurred and merged together over time, becoming vague outlines. She had thought she would recognise people as she came across them, but now realised that their individual features were not clear to her. But now she saw Gladys she knew it was her, although the years had not been all that kind. She was very glad she had instantly recognised Beatrice when she witnessed the scene outside the house all those weeks - months even - ago. How awful it would have been to have made a mistake! As much as she blamed the others for their involvement, and from what Maeve had said, for their attitude towards her mother, she had no wish to do more than get the main culprit to pay her dues. Others would, obviously, be hurt emotionally, but she could not dwell on that and it would only be fair, wouldn't it. Had she not been hurt emotionally?

She called across "Gladys, you had better come and say your goodbyes to Beatrice." Gladys stared at this schoolgirl. She could not equate the voice with the school girl - it was not a schoolgirl's voice. The voice she heard would not have been out of place from a teacher, a doctor, a …. a professional of some kind. It was adult, and dictatorial. It was cold and directing. She stared at her. Then almost by virtue of mind control by the girl, her eyes were pulled towards the now prone, and lifeless, bloody body that had been Beatrice. Gladys did not move - unbelieving and obviously distraught. Had it been a film, or a play, the script would have called for Gladys to scream and yell, but in reality what she did was freeze. She was unable to utter anything. She became a statue, with her mouth shaped in a scream but with no sound coming out. She made no attempt to approach, let alone, attack Helen. It was as though she really believed that some disembodied spirit had spoken to her, and had killed her daughter or that she was in the middle of some kind of hallucination. As though Helen was not even there. She was completely unable to equate Helen with the scene, with the voice, with the tragedy. At worst, the 'child' was merely an innocent spectator. Helen said, quite dispassionately, "Gladys, you had better go outside and see if you can find a policeman. Or use the phone at the bottom of the road. Go now. I will stay here." She found she had to physically push Gladys out of the door. The woman was still zombie-like and completely disbelieving of what she had seen; convinced she was somehow in a dream - a nightmare, even. But eventually, she did find her voice, and her feet, but instead of carrying on down the stairs, she flew back into the room and grabbed Helen by the shoulders and shook her as violently as she could, screeching at her and saying "Who was it? Who was it? What happened. What …… oh God, what was it! What happened …. Did something come through the window …. What in God's name happened!!"

Eventually, Helen found it necessary to go down the stairs herself, walk to the telephone box on the corner and calmly tell the responder that she had just stabbed somebody to death. She gave the address clearly and without any emotion, stating that she was returning to the house and would wait there until they arrived. It was true to say that they were inclined to believe that it was very likely a hoax or a malicious time waster, but given the seriousness of the matter, they were not really in a position to take the chance. *(In time, the telephone call and the bizarreness of it, were given as an indication that the girl was not, to put it in the vernacular - though that was not the way it was phrased in Court! - "all there!")*

Anyway, Helen returned to the house. Gladys was now slowly returning to some kind of sanity. She was now crying properly - sobbing - not screaming and hysterical. It still felt wrong to Helen that the woman was so 'reasonable' - not attacking her, blaming her, stabbing her, even. The knife was still there - very very very visibly there - not to mention a whole drawer full of weapons some ten feet away from her. But no. It seemed she still completely failed to register that this girl - this child, a total stranger - had for no reason at all, come to their home, fully prepared, and stuck a knife in her daughter ... and was now standing calmly by her side as though nothing had occurred.

Helen could not tolerate this lack of focus any longer, and was determined that before the police arrived, this woman - her aunt - should be made fully aware of who she was, why she was there, and hence why the whole thing was necessary. The enormous kitbag had been put down on the floor, and she tutted loudly as she bent down, released the drawstring and removed the bulky article which was inside. She shook quite violently the still disbelieving Gladys who was crouching down and cradling her daughter's head and murmuring to herself. Eventually by sheer inability to ignore the insistence of Helen, the distraught woman was forced to return to reality, and found herself staring at a fur coat. A very familiar fur coat. A fur coat she had never been able to forget. A fur coat she had seen in her nightmares many times. Looking now into the girl's eyes she knew. She no longer had to wonder why, or who. Those eyes were the eyes of her mother, Margaret Helen, shrewd eyes, vengeful eyes, hard and calculating eyes. This was Jimmy's girl - the little girl under the table watching, but not understanding, her mother die before her very eyes. Connie knew then that this day had been a long time coming, but it was as inevitable as day following night. This girl had their blood flowing through her veins. How could it have ended any differently? It had always been just a matter of time.

It would perpetuate. The others would never forgive her but Gladys had stayed with her mother during the many months that she was very ill, and when she finally died. They had spoken a lot in those times, and she knew that her mother had been troubled and ill at ease. She had spoken a lot about the 'old days', the family past, the family secrets. Gladys knew everything now. Though not the oldest, she had taken over the mantle of keeper of secrets like a baton from her mother. Unlike her mother, though, now that the past had resurrected itself again, she would not act as watchdog and problem solver. The past must be buried once and for all, and the future safeguarded by action not by permanent fire-fighting! The solution had to be permanent. She had to stop this perpetuating! She could not forget that the girl had killed her daughter - how could she. It would live with her forever. How could she just forgive her! But she understood! Oh God how well she understood! She needed to put a stop to it. Now, once and for all. Her mother, Maggie, had tried as best she could when she was alive, and the loosening of the ties within the family now that she was not there had helped matters, but it was just such an event as this that could undo all that. Now the family curse was in danger of resurrecting itself again. She would not let it. Somebody had to intervene. Too many people had died. More people than even she knew.

Chapter 15:   Time to pay the piper

Helen had left the front door open when she returned from the phone box, and it was not so very long - but it seemed like an age - before the sound of heavy boots were heard on the staircase. The first to enter the room, removing his helmet in some strange sort of courtesy gesture on entering a stranger's home, was a too young, very green humble beat bobby, very much out of his comfort zone. This poor - in the sense of unfortunate, as opposed to dilatory -   representative of the law was PC Clarke (needless to say, Nobby to his colleagues). He was just 23 and had been allowed out walking the beat following basic training only for the past nine months. That was preceded by two years' military service, which PC Clarke had endured but definitely not enjoyed in any way. During his time as a member of the Queen's armed forces, PC Clarke had done nothing at all exciting or noteworthy, except for the fact that he had been part of a group of young soldiers who had to be rescued when they got themselves completely lost during training manoeuvres on Salisbury Plain. This had made the papers - it being a slow news day - and consequently, both in the army, and now in the police force, he had found it difficult to live down. During his first week he had suffered the indignity of gibes and humiliation from his fellow cadets.   His confidence had been further sapped when, having thought he had made friends, and gained some kind of respect from his comrades, they had all gone out drinking to celebrate their completion of the course, prior to going their separate ways. Nobby was not a drinker, and it did not take long for the alcohol to go to his head. The next morning, he awoke in the doorway of a notorious brothel, and found that he had a crude map of Salisbury Plain and its environs tattooed on one forearm and the rough geography of Camden Town, including the Zoological gardens, on the other. They looked red and sore where they had been rubbed by his shirt and jacket sleeves, so quite apart from being an embarrassing reminder of his failings, he was in considerable discomfort! He had taken a long time to live any of this down, but had persevered and apart from having to permanently wear long sleeves and avoid swimming, the only other person who now regularly saw the offending designs was his wife, Jenny who had been his childhood sweetheart. Despite this inauspicious recommendation, he was academically at least average, and by no means a poor specimen of a man. He was fit, 6ft 1in, no criminal record and had no hint of any kind of indiscipline either at school or in the army, which was why he had passed muster and was accepted by the Metropolitan Police. Since being let loose on and the streets of North London, the worst thing he had had to confront had been a pickpocket brandishing a sweeping brush that he had grabbed off a market stall whilst being chased through a local market.

PC Clarke was followed by a WPC (obviously sent because some little girl had either gone doolally, or gone homicidal. Whichever way, young girls not being at all the province of young male policemen, Nobby had to be accompanied). While Nobby stood dumbfounded at the sight - not being used to murders, let alone one as 'homely' as this one, he was trying to remember the rule book, the procedure, to keep his head! The WPC, who was called Stansfield - to be precise, Carol Stansfield - went over and, in the manner that she had frequently used in her previous incarnation as an infant school trainee teacher, crouched down and took Helen's hand, asking solicitously "What's happened here then?" Even to her it sounded bald and inappropriate, but then the whole situation was inappropriate and, to say the least, unusual. The two members of the local constabulary had entered the house gingerly, somewhat excited, but hoping that they did not have to throw themselves at some homicidal maniac but this homicidal maniac - if one disregarded her very own telephone admission of guilt - seemed the least likely person in the whole city to have plunged a carving knife into the back of a seemingly ill-prepared woman, given that she was still half dressed and had obviously been caught unawares.

Neither PC Clarke, nor WPC Stansfield had come across anything remotely like this before, and it had certainly not been on the curriculum at Hendon, but both were practical people and fought hard against showing their horror or inadequacy. There being no telephone in the house, and not wishing to leave WPC alone, nor allow the culprit - unlikely as it seemed - to do further damage or make a run for it, Nobby Clarke went over to the window and opening it as wide as he could, he blew several long blasts on his police whistle to alert any other colleague who might happen to be in the vicinity. He knew this was obviously a matter for people better able and more qualified than himself to deal with, but in the meantime the responsibility was his to remember the protocol and, as he had been taught, 'contain the situation'. There being no immediate response to his whistling, except from alarmed and quizzical passers-by, he instructed Carol Stansfield to leave what she was doing, whether that was comforting or controlling the girl neither of them were sure, and go and telephone the police station and alert the detective division that they had a situation that needed more specialist attention.

By this time, Gladys had cleared her head somewhat, but was still surprisingly unable to attack, condemn or even speak against Helen. She knew what had happened - what the girl had done. She was hampered, though, by the fact that however much she, Gladys, was devastated by what had happened - what the girl, her niece, had done, had almost certainly just been a matter of time. Understanding the girl so well, even if not forgiving her, she knew that she had had no choice. She had to do what she had to do. How could it be any different. The family was the family was the family. The sins of the father must inevitably be inherited by the sons. But this was a supremely matriarchal family, so though the gender might be different, the principle was undoubtedly the same. Vengeance and hatred had been part of the family for years - probably generations - so how could this have ended any differently. But that was the thing, wasn't it! It probably had not ended. Might never end. More was the pity!

WPC Stansfield was somewhat reluctant to leave the house. She was not sure what she was afraid of. She could not really believe that the girl would suddenly jump up out of the calm and almost detached mood that she was in, and attack Nobby Clarke, or the other woman, but who could tell. It seemed completely impossible that she had viciously stabbed the dead woman, apparently unprovoked and without explanation, but by all accounts she had. But Carol had no option but to do as instructed. She was a lowly WPC and Nobby Clarke was a man, he had a bit more service under his belt, and she knew she had only been sent because of the child. So she went to the police box and rang the station, gave as much information as she knew, much of which the Desk Sergeant, Sergeant Carberry, sounded sceptical about. However, since it was obviously a murder - committed by somebody even if this silly girl, and the equally green and naive Nobby Clarke had got it arse about face about the responsible party - he passed on the information 'upstairs' and told the WPC to get back to the child and make sure she was all right and that nobody left the scene - particularly the other woman. Since Gladys was the only other person there, his money was on her as the culprit, after all how likely was it that this poor young girl went up to a perfect stranger in their own home and plunged a knife into them! No, take it from him. It was the other one. The child was either terrified or in shock.

Sergeant Carberry's reaction would set the scene for Helen's future dealings with the various levels of law enforcement. Even when it became absolutely beyond certain that she had, contrary to everybody's opinion, hopes and explanation, killed Beatrice, they all still retained a desire to protect her, to find mitigating circumstances and to see the reasons why. Much to her surprise, and indeed her chagrin, all attention turned to finding excuses for her rather than underlining the fact that, whatever the motivation, Beatrice was nonetheless just as dead.

When the detectives arrived expecting, as had Sergeant Carberry, to prove the stupidity of these rookie Woodentops' solution to the case, they were very soon aware that their scepticism had been misguided. The scene, the explanation, the reading of the facts was just as had been first intimated to them. The child had, it appeared, plunged a knife into this woman, who had obviously not provoked or even warded off this attack since she must have been half way into a tight fitting dress and so completely at the mercy of the girl. That being the case, the girl must have been deeply wronged in some way, because she was little more than a child, certainly not some kind of knife-wielding homicidal maniac! No there had to be more to this than met the eye. This woman must have done something to her. She obviously must have had it coming!

When they returned to the police station, with Helen, but without any kind of outward sign that she was a dangerous criminal, or a 'guilty party', they sat her in an empty office, rather than a cell, and gave her orange juice and chocolate biscuits. They left a WPC with her in case she got frightened or upset, certainly not in case this dangerous villain should try to escape or attack somebody. What a silly suggestion!

Then, when they began to look at the picture in detail, and realised that Beatrice had only recently been released from prison after serving a long sentence for murder, that put the whole thing into context! They had known that there must be more to it. The girl was obviously defending herself - despite what appeared to be the case at the house. After all the victim was a killer - only saved from hanging or a life sentence because she had a clever lawyer and a namby-pamby judge! The so-called attacker was a sweet very young schoolgirl - still in her school uniform, for God's sake - who was so traumatised by the whole experience that she really believed that she was to blame. How manipulative these scrotes can be! Heaven knows what the other old bitch had said to her before the plods arrived on the scene. She was probably terrified and unable to say anything - threatened, obviously, nothing could be clearer.

It was becoming a very trying situation for Helen. She had planned, she had prepared, she had pictured her life up to this point, and her hanging and oblivion after that. She had seen no need to make any contingency plans for afterwards. Afterwards would be short-lived and would take care of itself. How wrong could she be!

With Beatrice's 'sins' against her coming to light and with Gladys refusing to co-operate with the legal process, it was very perplexing and frustrating for the representatives of the law. It had to be remembered that the family had always had their own clear - if twisted and misguided - attitude towards 'the law'. On top of that, Gladys could perfectly understand - even in a bizarre way approve - of Helen. It was difficult for her because her own daughter had been the victim, but that consideration apart, Helen had done precisely the right thing! She could never, would never, cooperate to condemn her. She did have, though the dilemma of Susan. Like Helen, she saw the possibility - even the likelihood - of this vendetta going on for generations. But, she would have to sort that out herself. She did not need the Law to sort out family matters.

It was a shame that Lena was so poorly at the moment - the fags were always going to be the undoing of her! - and Connie seemed to be working all hours that God sent (ironically as a waitress at the Law Society - how bloody inappropriate was that!). The family had never had any truck with the law, and her mother would turn in her grave - apart from the fact that they were gathering a nice little collection of good quality cutlery and other odds and ends! But as for helping the Law to hang Helen, that Maggie would never have condoned. So the girl had gone about it arse about face, and it was obviously not ideal that Beatrice was dead, but two wrongs did not make a right! Beatrice had brought it on herself - silly cow - when she stuck the bloody knife in the Irish bitch. It was true, too, that she had been up her own Khyber since she got released - you would think she had come back from a bloody cruise, first class at that. She had wanted waiting on hand and foot, brought precious little into the house, and was an absolute useless role model for Susie. As for Sue, she hardly knew her mother, and by all appearances, liked her even less. No, daughter or not, truth to tell, Beatie was no great loss. That sounded harsh and unfeeling she knew, but she had got used to her being 'dead' to them for all those years she had been away. She was a silly little cow before she went away, but at least she was considerate and family minded. When she came home, she was still a silly cow, but was hard-nosed and insolent and too handy with her gob and her fists. They had always sorted out their own problems. She just had to protect Susan. This was the kind of feud that could run and run. It was up to her to keep a lid on it. She was not sure just how, but she had to some way or other.

PART THREE

Chapter 16: The rather too late intervention of psychiatry!

Helen had never denied her guilt. Helen tried to explain as best she could to the two nice detectives who came in to speak to her. She was getting very irritated because they did not seem to be taking her seriously - she thought they believed her, but somehow they had it in their heads that she was somehow the victim of circumstances and somebody had done something to her and she had to defend herself. In a way, of course, that was true. Somebody had done something to her, but not today, and she herself had never been in any danger - quite the reverse.

Helen decided to try and make them start from the beginning, and gave them as clear a picture of the family history as she could, which helped a bit, but in reality from what they were saying, it seemed that they knew much of that already. It was also true, though she did not know it, that even she only had part of the story. She just kept stressing that she had had no option. Justice had not been done before, so it was up to her to put matters right. Her biggest regret was not the act itself but the fact that she had misjudged and miss-researched the consequences. That they had to now endlessly dissect and analyse the whole thing was a waste of their time, and she had long since ventured into unknown territory. She was no longer within her comfort zone; she now had no well researched and rehearsed plan for these circumstances. This had not been foreseen at all. While she in reality felt eight years old again inside, confused and disillusioned, the detectives who had drawn the short straw and had been given the task of interviewing her, were marvelling at the composure, the detachment, the lack of any kind of obvious remorse or even fear. What was on the inside, had no way of advertising itself to the outside. Helen was, as usual, an island unto herself. Insular, introvert and impenetrable. She had seen the story as a simple one: Beatrice had killed her mother, without any justification, and was back with her daughter, when she, Helen, was not yet even out of school! Where was the justice in that!

Suddenly getting a boost of resolve and reaffirmation from her inward contemplation of the whys, wheres and whatfors, she sat up straighter and much to their alarm, and probably adding a certainty to their minds, that she was to say the least slightly unhinged (*"and who could blame her!" thought they*!) told them that she had assumed that she would just plead guilty and she would be hanged -

end of story! Hanged and gone. That was the fate she had counted on as part of a detailed and painstakingly enacted life plan since she was 12 years old.

They panicked then, and the powers that be made a decision to bring in the psychiatrists. Pass on the responsibility to somebody else! That was when I arrived on the scene.

So the case against Helen Collier was at face value cut and dried. Even Helen was saying she did it! There was an eyewitness to the murder and absolutely no getting away from the facts. Indeed, the girl was lobbying for execution herself (though at her age that was not even a likelihood - the days of hanging and deportation of children were, thankfully, long since gone). But she was definitely causing worries and embarrassment to the law enforcers who were trying as best they could, like Pontius Pilate, to wash their hands of the responsibility. 'Not on my head'! 'Let somebody else sort it!' 'Please!'

That somebody, then, was going to be me. After all, it sat less comfortably on jurors' and legal minds and hearts to execute or incarcerate for life a female; it was definitely less comfortable on jury and legal minds to execute or incarcerate for life a virtual child;

it was definitely less comfortable on jury and legal minds to execute or incarcerate for life a person who was a very damaged and maligned person. All of those described Helen.

People in general are quite easily swayed in their judgement. Even had Helen been older, that is over the 'hanging' age (since we are talking prior to the abolition of the death penalty in the UK) it was probably, on the face of it, unlikely that she would have got her wish. When the culprit was a pretty, very young, intelligent, well-spoken and polite schoolgirl it would have been nigh on impossible…. regardless of absolutely cast-iron evidence of guilt!
It had happened, of course. Females had been hanged; young people had been hanged, though 18 was probably the earliest that jurors and judges found it comfortable to recommend it. And usually only then when they were what people considered 'yobs', 'thugs' or 'wrong 'uns!'

So, that was the crux of the problem and why I was engaged to help her - and the Courts. The Courts were concerned that she - and she would not be the first - was unstable and was merely an exhibitionist who was misguidedly angling for a kind of 'assisted suicide'. For my part, I was equally anxious on her behalf since she was virtually a child. Helen was 16, so ironically old enough to marry, though not old enough to vote, and she was very 'together' and unemotional, but in truth, she was little more than a child just the same. Had it been today, of course, I would have been better informed. Writing now, in more enlightened times, I would have been able to give a much more fancy - though perhaps somewhat glibber - diagnosis. But we are talking 1957 and the word 'Autistic', let alone 'Asperger's', may well have been on some clever researcher's radar, but for the world at large, even us medical professionals, were relatively unfamiliar with those concepts. Even now, though, I am - between thee and me - of the opinion that though I would have probably used that excuse for Helen, in my heart of hearts I am not really certain that it would have been the truth. Particularly after talking to her relatives. I think she was a very troubled and emotionally damaged girl and had she committed her crime as a real adult, she would probably have been hanged and she would have welcomed that. She somehow had mapped out her life to that end. At the time I did not think she was a danger to others, though in the light of conversations with others, there were times when I doubted my own confidence in that fact. At the time, I believed that unless she found another Joan of Arc cause to follow all would be perfectly well.

So back to Helen's story as told to me, during those long and surprisingly unemotional sessions during which I tried in vain to find a reason why the Courts should not lock her up for life. I should say early on, in case people get either disappointed or jubilant depending upon how they take to or take against her that I singularly failed and Helen was ultimately consigned originally to Cragmoor and latterly to Prestbury 'at Her Majesty's Pleasure'. She remains an inmate even now, visited frequently by people who still love her - and more surprisingly by one or two who owe her no favours. She is content and since she is probably/possibly not a danger any longer to anybody, she may be released within the next year or two - though she is causing consternation because she is so difficult to read; she gives nothing; she makes no demands either for release, or privileges, or even attention. The unknown, the unfathomable, are always greater challenges than the wheeler dealers, the manipulators, to a trained eye, because one is permanently faced with the dilemma 'what if?' Nobody wants to be the one to take the chance. So nobody does. And Helen does not request. Helen does not plead. Helen does not make any case on her own behalf for her release. Her Majesty's Pleasure in Helen's case, seems to be more at Helen's Pleasure. She has replaced her death wish for a life wish - a life behind bars.

Some of the background detail I got from speaking with her father and her stepmother, as well as from her surrogate parents, Maeve and Kevin Clarkin, with whom she had spent much of her early years and who had first-hand information as close friends and confidantes of Helen's mother, Elizabeth. *(Though much of their information relating to the Collier family was through the eyes and storytelling of Elizabeth, they had met the family once, at the wedding. They had been easily able to identify each and every one, since Elizabeth had described them, mimicking their accents and their mannerisms to a T during her frequent visits to the Clarkin household while she was courting James).* Surprisingly, I also spoke at length to Gladys - the eye witness, the mother of the original killer, and the ultimate victim - after the sentence had been decided upon. Despite the fact that it had been a traumatic and upsetting time for all - not least Gladys and James - all were most forthcoming and more numbingly honest than I could ever have expected. I believe, then, this to be as clear and true a picture of the events and their psychological causes and effects as it is possible to interpret.

I have also allowed Helen herself a voice in the conclusion of this book, since she was anxious that I did not paint her in anything but a guilty light, and that I did not in any way massage the truth! She is still uncomfortable with the account to some extent, and in particular is disturbed by her aunt's apparent 'understanding' and forgiveness evidenced by her frequent visits to see her. She first of all accepted this as a kind of penance, believing Gladys to be visiting in order to remind her constantly of what she had done - the grief she had caused her and she was content with this, accepting her 'punishment'. But after a while, it became evident that Gladys, for some reason, was merely sorrowful that events had played out as they had - all of the events, Helen's loss no less than her own - and that she was to a large degree relatively unaffected by the actual death of her daughter, Beatrice. *(Both women, like previous generations of the Collier family, seem to have a similar inability to feel distress in the conventional sense. They are less than 'normally' affected by death and loss, though they have a keen sense of 'payback' and retribution. With Gladys, I believe, from my discussions with her, she was greatly affected by the 'family confessions' passed on to her before her mother's death, and from receiving the baton to try to protect and prevent tragedy rather than maintain the unfortunate disregard of human life that their ancestors had been only too guilty of).*

Helen at first was less disheartened at being confined than the fact that she was to remain alive, considering this to be some kind of failure on her part - part of the plan that she had failed to bring to fruition. Though I do not believe that she is capable of suicide - I have never believed that she did what she did simply to achieve that end - obviously the staff within the establishment cannot take that risk, and certainly cannot take my word for it! So she remains alive, and will probably remain so, since her safety is monitored constantly and her health is far better protected by others than by herself.

I have tried to write this report as a proper story, not a factual account, though it is as accurate and 'professional' as can make it without it being dull as ditch-water, since it was as much intended as an interesting read as much as a means of documenting the facts.

I kept a watching brief on Helen over the years, re-interviewing her at regular intervals, partly because of my duty of care to both her and Society at large, but, I must confess also out of curiosity and professional interest. She was, for me anyway, unique, and I was reluctant to put the pencil down and walk away.

The interview notes recorded below were made after a good few years - perhaps seven or eight - when Helen was in her mid-twenties. She was always perfectly polite and terrifyingly self-analytical.

She analysed herself in an infinitely more insightful and cold-blooded way than I ever did. What follows, then, on separate pages, are the words of the girl - now woman - Helen Collier. I have kept them as they were spoken, and interrupted and/or interpreted them very little, since they speak for themselves though I have made one note to myself that so much of the story, so many of the phrases, seem to be given almost by rote, as though they have been practised frequently. This I have subsequently confirmed to be fact, since Helen herself has told me that she had planned, and imagined all or most of the events long before they occurred - apart from the aftermath, the sympathy, the gentleness even, that she received from all quarters. She had imagined quite the reverse: her utter condemnation, and a quick trial, and that she would be 'hanged by the neck until she be dead'. That was the end she foresaw, which is why much of the interview spoken by her seems as though she is speaking lines from a play - a rehearsed script. It indeed was rehearsed - apart from the outcome, which she still fails to understand and much less appreciate.

Chapter 17: The recorded thoughts of Helen Collier, 8 years into her sentence.

"I find it necessary to try to see my family as 'normal' and the circumstances surrounding them as 'commonplace'. That, I hope, might make me seem less justified and more culpable. I find it difficult in here, behind locked doors. Not difficult to know why I am here; not difficult to understand why I did what I did. Despite what people may think to the contrary, believe me, I am completely compos mentis and understood and understand fully my actions and the consequences of them both on myself and more importantly on others. (**Note from psychiatrist: Rehearsed speech. Has thought about this, planned it, including the inevitable outcome!**) *What, though, is a shock and completely beyond my comprehension is the fact that everybody else thinks that it was 'understandable'. That what I did was not quite justified, but certainly in some way excusable! Everybody - even those who should hate me - seems sympathetic and understanding. Obviously they all think of me as much sinned against as sinning! So here I am not in an unmarked and spat upon grave, not even a prison cell, but in this hospital, albeit a special hospital - not quite your NHS local one! I know*

they keep me separate - one might even say segregated - but that is the closest they come to punishing me.

For many years, absolutely nothing was said about my mother. My father was a good man, a caring man, but a very private person. He was not demonstrative or even easy to talk to. I loved him, and I know he loved me, but we never voiced these emotions nor, I suppose, expected them to be voiced.

Once I found his box of newspaper cuttings, and Maeve showed me the other box of things which my father had given to her because he could not bear to see them, obviously I started to understand him and his isolation more. He had not only lost my mother, but he had, by that very circumstance, lost his entire family too - except me, and I was not at all easy to love or live with. From his joy and ease in the company of Sofia and the twins, I know that he was not, by nature, so guarded and miserly with his affection: I perhaps wrong him there because it was not his affection - I am sure he always loved me - it was the showing of that affection that he and I had been lacking.

I think, perhaps, from reading (upside down, and without their approval!) some of the notes of the various trick cyclists that have been to see me over the years, that I do have some kind of 'kink' or bad wiring in my brain that makes me a bit of a lame duck emotionally, but I really don't believe that my Dad was. If my 'deficiency' was an accident of birth, his was definitely the result of a deliberate and cowardly act which deprived him in one fell swoop of his wife, his family, and his happiness.

My Aunt Gladys has been to see me many times since I arrived here. I find that strange and - I have to admit it - somewhat distasteful. I killed her daughter! Why then does she act as though it is nothing! We don't talk about it. We don't talk about anything much - the weather, the news, the latest styles or Top Ten records. She has though - and I am glad - seemed to have forged some kind of reconciliation with Dad. I guess I did him a favour since she evidently sees the death of Beatrice as providing a balance – 'Even Stevens', maybe!

It doesn't make any sense! Why should I be forgiven? Why should I be pitied! I knew precisely what I was doing. I'd certainly do it again! I might go to hell, but I believe I would do it again! BUT when all's said and done, a woman is dead! Susan has no mother. Like I had no mother. So with our family, the cycle could repeat itself, perhaps endlessly.

End of interview

Little did Helen know, when she recorded the final statement in the recording above, how close to the mark she was.

I have also had the opportunity, as part of my original investigation and latterly, I have to admit, because of my near-obsession with the case, interviewed the other people involved - even those on the periphery: Susan, Gladys, James Collier, Connie/Lena (very briefly – they were not very forthcoming!) Sofia, Maeve, Kevin, and some of the older Clarkin children. After several years, it is easier to get a clearer picture from them all - they are less traumatised by the actual events, and Helen's physical removal from the scene makes it easier for them to put their feelings and memories into words. Of all of them, perhaps Susan is the most concerning. She seems completely unmoved by much of it. She states in quite a hard, even blasé, fashion that she never really knew her mother; she never really liked her mother and though she thought it was a 'shame' that she had died in the way she did, 'what goes around, comes around' she supposed!

Maeve - and perhaps even more so Kevin - seem to have had the best chance to study and perhaps understand Helen, but both had been brought up in large, quirky, independent families.   Families where infants, toddlers, children, adolescents, young adults and ultimately grown adults more or less brought themselves up.   They had each had siblings - and indeed close and not so close relatives - who had been somewhat 'individualistic' and even 'odd' to the outside world.   It was just the rich tapestry of Irish life!   The abnormal was perhaps more normal!   Maeve also had the advantage of knowing the background and make-up of Elizabeth's family - Helen's maternal history - in Ireland, since she was a childhood friend of one of Elizabeth's sisters and they had all been raised in a very small town, little more than a village by London standards, and she had known the truths, the half-truths and the mere rumours and suspicions that had surrounded the family over generations.   The family was perhaps a bit more colourful than many, and had provided the locals with many a fireside gossip and debate over the years.   They had a chequered history, with three of the maternal great uncles having decided that America beckoned following the fatal shooting of a landowner - a tyrant by all accounts, but none the less dead for all that.   The men were suspected and were initially questioned by the representatives of the British Crown, but were copiously alibied by almost too many neighbours who in their desperation to be helpful all contradicted each other. When that seemed to be causing more harm than good, they moved on to a new strategy. By harbouring the men, working together to thwart the investigation, and enlisting the strategic nous and network of the local activists, the men managed to reach the nearest departure point and blend in with the many other Irish emigrants seeking a better life and a brighter future across the Atlantic. So the men were never tried, and hence not convicted, but there was, apparently, little doubt amongst their neighbours of their guilt - or as they considered it their sacrifice - since they were hailed as heroes by their peers. The family history, too, was one of constant rifts and fallings out, with brothers and sisters not talking to one another for years, or indeed unto death, in some cases. Many family members either died very young - frequently under tragic circumstances - or lived exceptionally long lives, though scattered to the four winds, and making little or no contact with one another over the years and the miles. Maeve described them as super intelligent and remarkably well read and educated, handsome and athletic, but all, very quick to anger, long to hold a grudge, and swift to take offence. Kevin had not known the family, so had only been able to judge from his relatively brief acquaintance with Elizabeth herself. He found her good company, witty, a good cook "which helps a lot, doesn't it!" -, attractive, but 'deep'. He was, he said, quite cagey around her and careful not to get on her bad side! But he laughed and added that that could be because he was afraid of Maeve's right hook! Kevin often tried to create the impression that he had an eye for the women, but truth be told, with or without her 'right hook' he adored Maeve, and despite their almost constant castigating of each other when others were around, she idolised him in return.

Maeve and Kevin had also had some opportunity - though he was not a very forthcoming or emotional person - of spending time with James after he returned from the War, and after he left his family home and became sole guardian of Helen. He had been clearly fond of Elizabeth, and had been devastated, first of all by her absence and the mystery that surrounded that, and then even more so by the subsequent events surrounding not only her death, but the trial and the inevitable alienation from his own family as a result. They liked him, but were more than happy when he met and married Sofia and eventually had the twins, because he was not an easy person to be around. He was introvert and overly polite. He was polite but not 'good' company. Not drinker, not a social animal. Kevin had tried hard, but they were as different as chalk and cheese, and it was a Godsend when he had married Sofia. After that, they had seen less of him - as a couple - though Maeve visited to help Sofia with the twins - but when they did meet up, the whole situation was more relaxed and James was comfortable in his own skin and seemed at peace. Until, that is, he discovered that Beatrice had been released and was living back in his old house. That had dealt him a bit of a blow and it was as much as all of them could do to distract him and get his mind off it. Had it not been for his obvious joy in his twin baby sons, then there is no doubt in the minds of Maeve - and even more so Kevin, who worked with him - that he would have reverted to the James of old and gone in on himself again.

Maeve had discovered some months before the death of Beatrice that her 'treasure box' - with the cuttings, the brooch, the coat and other keepsakes and mementos of Elizabeth - had gone missing. She knew, of course, who had taken it. She had seen Helen many times eyeing the box, and once or twice she had come across her looking through the contents before surreptitiously returning it to its hiding place. She had considered that the box was the property of Helen in any case, and as the girl had clearly seen the cuttings many times before, she did not see it as wrong that she should take it - she would, of course, have rather she spoke about it before taking it, but they had got used over the years to Helen and she did not communicate the way that anybody else communicated. She would never have considered it necessary to 'ask permission' she would have rightly identified it as the property of her mother, and therefore hers as of right. Needless to say Maeve had never in a million years imagined just what the taking of that box signified, nor where that coat might end up once it left her house.

I also spoke at length to James, and to Sofia also. They had both blamed themselves for a long time that they had not taken into consideration the fact that Helen might overhear them when they were speaking about Beatrice being out of prison and back in the neighbourhood. Both Sofia, and Maeve - and in time, even myself - had tried to persuade him that Helen's 'plan' and intention was formed long before that fateful night, and it had only been a question of when. If Helen had not heard of Beatrice's return from him, she would have learned of it some other way because sooner or later somebody at school, or in the local shops, or on the bus, or anywhere would have mentioned it. The neighbourhood was full of people who had lived around those streets for generations, and nothing was really secret from them. 'They were not thoughtless people, by and large, so people more often than not held their tongues, exercised discretion, but it only took a careless word in the privacy of somebody's own home, in front of a schoolmate or acquaintance of Helen, for the cat to be out of the bag. Eventually, also, when she thought the sentence as imposed was more or less up, she would have enquired and that that would have made it worse. By then, Helen would have been older, and for all he knew, she might have been hanged - because for certain she would still have gone ahead with her task. Nothing and nobody was going to dissuade her.

James was glad to talk me about his guilt and his concerns as to whether his parenting - or in his view lack of it - had condemned Helen to her present plight. He was very anxious because now he was involved in the day to day routine of married life and hands on parenting of his twins, he saw only too clearly how different that was from the life that he and Helen had led. He was convinced that his lack of involvement in her life, and his selfish concentration on his own sadness and resentment had influenced her course of action and her obvious depression. It was impossible for me to reassure him totally about this, since to some degree it most certainly had not helped, but I did try to reassure him that he had done nothing out of malice or negligence and that he should not blame himself. I wanted to add 'entirely' but considered that not to be helpful in the circumstances, and since he was not a client or a patient, but merely a source of research in his daughter's case, it was perhaps not my place to go down that route.

My words only seemed to convince him that his real 'sins' and failings then must have been much earlier and that if he had been less engrossed in his own unhappiness, he might have seen that she needed him more. I seemed too harsh to tell him that I believed that his daughter's fate could have been altered, but that it was easy for people to be wise after the event. The poor man had lost enough without me putting the boot in. And, indeed, having spoken subsequently to Gladys, perhaps I am wrong! Perhaps the die was cast many generations back through the years. Certainly Maggie Collier believed that to be true! She had once been regarded as the Oracle.

My most enlightening interview then was with Gladys. I had been intrigued - and encouraged - that Gladys had taken to visiting Helen regularly, which on face of it seemed somewhat bizarre, but then nothing in the case had been 'normal'!

It was from Gladys in a very honest and frank 'confession' that I learned how and why Elizabeth had really died. I learned for the first time that the young Helen had witnessed her mother's murder, and that Gladys too had witnessed her own daughter wielding the knife and striking the fatal blow.

She described with a clarity and detail born out of relief and remorse after so many years of hiding the truth how Connie and she had taken the body in the pram, and how they had discussed the possibility of trying to pass off the death as the result of enemy action.

She had then for the first time explained why her mother, Maggie, had been perpetually watchful over the family, because theirs was a very unhappy - not to say catastrophic history.

The reason that Maggie insisted on the children living under her roof was that in the generations that had preceded theirs, at least three of their ancestors had been guilty of murder - one of more than one murder!   She knew this for a fact, by word of mouth passed down, though none of them had ever been suspected, detected or punished.

At least two of Maggie's great aunts and one great great aunt, had poisoned children (and others) for insurance money - one of them had claimed on at least two children.   Her great grandmother had claimed on the death of her husband, a daughter in law, and even a lodger who had been staying with them at the time, and who she had taken out insurance on when she found he was enticing her young son into his room for what she believed to be none too savoury a purpose. It turned out the 'none too savoury purpose' was that the poor chap, who missed his family far away, had nobody to play chess with him, and was convinced that the boy had an aptitude for it!

All of this had seemed to me somewhat difficult to believe, and there seemed to be no easy way of proving it - but then, I suppose no way of disproving it either - but it was clear that Gladys had believed it when Maggie, practically on her deathbed, had told her, and had explained the reason why the children had had to live with her, and why she was so careful about them. It was clear that such tales had coloured the behaviour of their entire household for all of their lives.

At the time I had no real knowledge as to whether any of this was fact or fiction. Was this just Maggie's way of keeping hold of her grandchildren and getting her way? From talking with Gladys, I do believe now that she, Gladys, believed it, and also accepted that Maggie truly considered them all to be in danger of succumbing to the 'murder gene' either as killer or victim. *(I have to admit to having a problem with this, in retrospect! It did seem to me, when I spoke to Gladys following the revelations of Maggie before she died, that she was genuinely surprised and even horrified at what she heard. However, I also have to take into account the fact that she herself, Gladys, had suffered several 'miscarriages' and 'lost' two babies at birth, or soon after? Coincidence? I acknowledge that in earlier times miscarriages, still births, infant mortality was far more common, so perhaps .... but if it was 'perhaps' for Gladys, was it also then 'perhaps' for all of the other Clements who were being tarred with the 'pernicious gene' brush!*

She was either a very good liar or actress, or they were real tragedies rather than convenient and engineered events. It is one of the mysteries, that even by the end of this tale, I cannot promise that I shall have reached an opinion on - I apologise in advance for this failing).

It is historical fact that there were many women in those times who did murder people, including children, for a few shillings of insurance money. Some of them, unlike Maggie's ancestors, actually got caught and were hanged for it. Her story seemed to have centred around Maggie's own line, that is the Clements (her maiden name) so one could either presume that the Clements were more canny than others, or that the insurance company involved was less diligent, or Maggie had been either malicious or gullible. Were they more 'canny' or was Maggie living in phantasy land. I just do not know.

Certainly Gladys, well-schooled by her mother, had rationalised the awful and tragic circumstances of first Elizabeth's death, and subsequently Beatrice's death, by putting them both down to 'genetics'. Helen had had no more choice than Beatrice had had apparently! They were both born to murder. Like they were born with a hearing defect or a propensity to Stroke or heart attack! Gladys had just to accept the doctrine of her mother, Margaret Helena, and be glad that both her other surviving children were boys, since, according to the oracle, the affliction only affected the female of the species in the family. Apparently Maggie had considered herself to be 'special' because though she most certainly might have been tainted by the 'evil gene', she had been 'spared'. Moreover, she had been given the special and unique responsibility of 'knowing' and 'preventing' and 'protecting' the family. *(I am seriously sorry that I never had the opportunity of properly interviewing Margaret Helena Collier herself, since she was obviously an extraordinary person. But was she mad as a hatter or Joan of Arc? Perhaps a Freudian analogy because Joan of Arc was likely suffering from some kind of mental health problem too!).*

So, I am sorry to leave people without real answers. I would have preferred to be definite and give a senior psychiatrist with 33 years' experience authoritative diagnosis, but I just cannot. The only two actual murders within the Clement/Collier family that I can personally comment on are those of Elizabeth Collier and Beatrice Collier. Those I truly believe were straightforward to judge: pure and simple anger for murder one, and pure and simple revenge for murder two. Nothing more earth-shattering than that! No family curses; no murderous genes; no historical excuses. Sorry Maggie I think you may have spent your entire life trying to prevent catastrophes that might never have happened, and in doing so, caused the very disaster that you had sought to guard against.

Helen remains in secure surroundings. It is difficult to give any kind of assurance that she will be released any time soon - or at all - since she does not make any effort to help herself and to persuade the decision makers that she is safe to release.

Gladys visits her frequently. I believe that she genuinely visits because she feels that Helen was also a victim, and that she is a family member - warts and all, and that she has, somehow, taken a hit for them all! She has also made her peace with her brother, James, though this is only in its infancy, and it is unlikely that James will cast aside the past, since he believes completely that though Beatrice struck the blow, the rest of the family - his mother, his sisters and his niece were all responsible and he had expected them to look after his wife in his absence. They had not just failed to protect her; they had destroyed her themselves. They had betrayed him and taken from him and Helen what could not be replaced. They had not only taken away his wife, Helen's mother, but they had done that as she watched, and so caused her to sacrifice her own life in order to avenge her mother. They could not have done anything worse if they had stabbed him instead.

All but two of Maeve and Kevin's children had grown up and had scattered - two to university, one to the United States, one backpacking around the world, one remaining in London, and one living with Maeve's parents in County Tipperary who were getting elderly and were glad to her company and help around the small - holding. Their parents returned home to Ireland when Kevin's father died and left him the family farm. Kevin was no farmer, however, and having rented out the land, he and Maeve had opened up a guesthouse and restaurant in the heart of County Cork which was doing well. Maeve wrote to Helen frequently, and promised her that she had a home with them just as soon as she was free to come to Ireland.

Following is the story as told to Gladys by Maggie just before she died. I have tried to corroborate what I can, and to add my own information - or as much as I have been able to glean from various explorations I have undertaken.   I have not found it easy, and I wish I could say I have done this for Helen, or even Gladys and Susan, but in truth, I have just got myself obsessed. Obsessed with proving or disproving the truth behind Maggie's 'concerns'; obsessed with discovering whether it is possible for such a thing to happen, for a 'murder gene' to pass down the line – and in particular down the female line only.   Call me a nosy old woman, but surely that is something that needs to be understood?

PART FOUR

Chapter 18: Family Secrets

First, because it is always useful to 'set the scene' let me offer some kind of 'comment' or route map through Margaret Helen's (Maggie's!) mind – not especially as an expert, a psychiatrist, but using my newly acquired passion, as a genealogist. Let it be known, however, that prior to this undertaking, and before my retirement, I had little interest, and indeed little time or patience, to think the individual's family tree was worth devoting several hours and many pounds to discover. Their own individual 'past' and influences certainly were profoundly relevant, but the antics of their great great grandmother and historical relations were not really on my curriculum! I had delved precious little into my own antecedents, let alone somebody else's! But there you have it, the case had me hooked – even in my dotage and when it mattered not a jot to anybody – least of all Helen. She would have been decidedly underwhelmed if the powers that be had decided to give her back her liberty.

I have decided, since I need to make this 'research' at least seem to have been done out of professional interest, rather than just nosiness and curiosity, to base all of my concentration on how the family dynamics have impacted on Helen. How they might have led her inevitably to her present predicament. Ah, there's the rub! Was it inevitable? That is where Maggie's 'death bed' confession, and Helen's actions collide and provide the cornerstone of my concentrated efforts – almost through compulsion – over the next decade or more! I have got to know her over the years, first as an 'assessor', then as an 'interested party' and latterly, I have to admit, as a kind of surrogate mother. I have never had children myself – and cannot say that for most of my life I have found that a sadness – but there is something more than fascinating about Helen. There is something that makes a person feel empathy and 'involvement' despite the horror of it all; despite the fact that it seems completely - to use a layman's term, but one that perhaps is as descriptive as any other - 'crackers'! She has at no point sought any such understanding and would most certainly run a mile from any demonstration of such unsolicited and definitely unwelcome pity. Such a damaged person, such a wasted life, such a loss to society.

I should add, before we all get maudlin, that Helen herself sees none of this. She is the most 'together' person I have ever met. She is perfectly content in her skin and has no regrets or longings. She is and was a model prisoner and gave nobody any trouble whatsoever, apart from when well-meaning and forward-thinking decision-makers decided that it was both safe and humane to move her to less secure, so less daunting, surroundings. They tried this twice, with similar outcomes.

She had reacted first of all by protesting in a measured fashion, explaining her views. When that failed, she made two attempts on her own life in order to underline her disapproval. First of all, (ironic, I thought, given her original planning in the early days!) she made a serious attempt to hang herself with a knitted scarf that she had been allowed to make during recreation and which somebody had forgotten to retrieve from her before she returned to her 'cell'. That was the problem, following the move, since she found it seriously misleading to use the word 'cell' about her new accommodation. *(Not that I was on the scene to register my views, being well and truly retired by that time ... In any case I think there would have been little chance of my views being listened to! They had failed to understand that she had no fear of death, she was protesting, but would have been just as content had they not heeded her views, to proceed with the alternative).* In case this seems to counteract my assertion that she is content and 'together', I should add that her one 'hang up' seems to be the fact that everybody thinks she is somehow the victim rather than the perpetrator. That has always been her stance – from her very early days when she had built into her plan her own execution. Nobody could have been more let down, it seemed from talking to her, at that time than Helen herself that she was essentially seen as somehow 'justified', that they had to punish her because people could not just go around murdering others, but that it somehow went against the grain to do so.

So the reason for her aggravation, and hence her drastic action was based on her strict idea that she deserved punishment rather than 'mollycoddling'. When the powers that be decided to move her to more salubrious surroundings with a less restrictive regime this just reinforced her let down with the world that they were 'soft' and 'namby-pamby'. Her new 'cell' was a pleasant enough room – small certainly and locked naturally – but with some comfort-providing features but it was not quite the four walls and a steel door with a spy hole variety that we might conjure up in our own minds when we hear the word 'cell' nor was it what Helen believed that she deserved. With the attempted hanging, she was, of course, discovered in good time and first of all efforts were doubled to ensure such opportunities were not offered to her again. But they decided to persevere and she was not given her way and not returned to the 'austerity' of her previous surroundings as she had so graphically requested.

The other protest was more a battle of wills, the original plan having not succeeded. She refused food and water, and any kind of cooperation or communication. Though force feeding may well have been OK for the suffragettes many years before, (and in subsequent years, but long after, the H-block prisoners in Northern Ireland) people were squeamish about using such tactics on a person who had been declared sufficiently mentally unsound by the Courts to be in an 'hospital' albeit a very forbidding one, rather than a common or garden maximum security prison. There had been a lot of sympathy at the time of her 'trial' (which bore out Helen's own complaints about the system!) from the general public, and though a lot of time had elapsed, the authorities did not want to wake up the sleeping giant and bring the wrath of public opinion down of on them for being heavy-handed and inhumane. That time she got her way and the hospital decided it was just not able to cope with somebody of her particular difficulties. They had been further helped in this decision by the not too subtle threat by Helen that next time she would not harm herself, but somebody else, most likely one of her fellow 'patients'. Despite their surprise, since she had always been a particularly non-aggressive and compliant inmate, they were not really in a position to decide that this was an empty threat. She had killed once before in an unprovoked attack out of the blue. She was 'a strange one' certainly, who had not really benefitted from any kind of psychiatric help over the years. Though she had not killed anybody else, thank God, her demeanour and attitude had remained substantially the same: introvert, brooding, non-reactionary.   She still seemed entirely devoid of any kind of remorse or even understanding that her action had been anything other than inevitable.   Wrong, certainly, but inescapable. She was not influenced by any kind of promise of freedom (quite the reverse in fact) nor did she show any signs of reacting to threats or promises of worse to come.   Visiting and on-staff psychiatrists to the various establishments over the years had most often used the phrases 'vacant', 'emotionally detached', 'de-sensitised', 'emotionless'.   In layman's terms, I guess, she was a 'shell'. She was going through the motions of living, but had long since 'died'.   If that makes you think of a zombie – that is a dead person walking – that is not too bad a comparison, but she was not – well to me anyway – frightening or 'horrific'.   Her outward appearance was not at all alarming, it was just that she was dead behind her eyes and her 'mood' was always the same: polite but aloof, non-inclusive, she 'gave' nothing, she made no efforts to please.

The following then are the 'facts' as told by Margaret.   The people she speaks about really did exist.   The 'deaths' really did, as far as I can ascertain, take place, but the facts behind those deaths are only capable of judgement by conjecture and supposition – guesswork, really! The era was minus a health service, an affordable availability of medicines and medical care. Without our modern notions and concentration on 'health and safety', immunisation, antibiotics, penicillin, etc. They were different times. Times of completely different dangers, life expectancies and expectations. Judge for yourselves. Because of the financial aspects, though, I was left at least suspicious about some of the events, so was at least left with an open mind. There is, I am sure you will agree, certainly some cause for sympathy with Maggie and her quest to protect the young from their elders!

Anyway, below is Margaret's own 'family history'. As for my own view, I have waivered backwards and forwards, but now, from my research, for whatever reason, I have become more understanding of her doctrine, and see it less as a means of controlling her daughters, as an attempt to outwit history and to pit her wits against the family curse – even if it was an imagined demon she was fighting!

My three conflicting reactions on first listening to Gladys retelling the story were: a) to marvel that she found it possible to relate this decidedly unflattering family history to a relative stranger; b) to consider that she was either embroidering or making the whole thing up out of some kind of desire to be 'different', 'colourful', 'dark and mysterious'; c) to wonder, if it was by some horrendous chance true and factual, how damaged was she already, and how much more damage had this new responsibility for the secrets of the family done to her?

MAGGIE'S DEATHBED TALE

According to Maggie, as delivered before she died, and to me through the mouthpiece of Gladys, the background of the Clement family would seem not just callous and amoral, but alarmingly driven and consumed with self-interest and greed.

Rebecca Johanna Clement, Margaret Helen Collier nee Clement's great great grandmother was allegedly responsible for the death by arsenic poisoning of at least four of her 8 children. Two other sons died under peculiar circumstances, which could have been engineered or could have been genuine accidents around the home.

George, when he was 5, accidentally fell into a fire pit that his mother had dug in order to burn bedding that she considered might be contaminated after the death of her first husband who had apparently died of smallpox whilst at sea, but whom she felt might have left traces of the disease behind him! Edward, 2, fell into an old dry well when he apparently tried to retrieve a lost toy. She was never charged with any of these deaths - neither the 'strange' nor the 'tragic'. She lived at a time when such 'losses' were taken as part of life and when human life seems to have been cheap in the extreme. *(I can confirm the actual births and deaths from the records, but obviously none of the deaths are officially recorded as 'smothered' or 'poisoned'! The 'arsenic' poisonings, for instance, were officially put down to 'influenza'. The fall was 'accidental death' due to a fall. The fire incident, 'accidental death' by burning.)*

According to Maggie, at least one of Rebecca's surviving daughters, was even more creative than Rebecca, extending her 'end of life' service to people outside the family also when she decided to rent out one of her rooms. In case that sounds like a really inventive and entrepreneurial thing to do in its own right, it should be acknowledged that the tiny two storey house, of which she only had the lower floor, comprised little more than a scullery, a small cramped main room with an open fire used for all the cooking and everything else, and one other adjoining room in which, when no 'lodger' was in residence, the entire family of mother, the remaining two sons and one daughter normally slept. Each 'lodger' was never around for very long. Their health deteriorated alarmingly quickly once in residence (having handed over rent money in advance) much to the overwhelming distress of their landlady who cried copious tears each time, but who counted the insurance pay-out, and re-let the room again once the coffers started to look low. She was always happy to share a cup of tea with the insurance agent, who was equally pleased to make another sale, even if his company must have been less enthralled at the rate at which they were needing to make payments for tragedies.

Maggie believed that there was a 'murder gene' passing down through the generations of the Clement women. She had been told of it by her mother when she was dying, and though she had not really believed it, she had then started to look again at what she herself had witnessed through different eyes, and had started to wonder, and give it more respect. She had been, she said, 'put on her guard' when she considered that two of her sisters 'lost' children under strange circumstances; she had had cousins that had 'died' young, and then – and Gladys was to keep it strictly to herself and not mention it to her, and wake the sleeping lion! – Lena had a baby who died very suddenly and, it seemed to Maggie, without causing all that much loss or grief to his mother! Off she went, allegedly, face full of make-up, off on the town and living it up like nothing had happened!

So that was Maggie's 'secret'. One which, according to Gladys, she genuinely believed and had felt that a duty had been given to her, by her own mother, to protect her grandchildren from their own mothers … bizarre? certainly. Deranged? possibly. True? Who knows!

I have made every effort to research the family background and to confirm whether Margaret Helen Collier nee Clement was: a) a person with a vivid imagination; b) a woman who would use any and every means to keep her grandchildren under her roof; c) a woman who was mentally deranged and genuinely but groundlessly fearful of elements within her family genetics which put her grandchildren in mortal danger of their lives; or d) a woman who was sane, sensible and was acting in the true interests of her grandchildren because, bizarre as it seemed, there actually was a pernicious gene within her family's genetic make-up which really did truly put their lives in jeopardy.

I am not sure whether I have proved or disproved any of the above – and all may be true to some extent, but certainly, studying the Clement family tree as best I can, there are worrying aspects of the history which lead me to believe that Maggie was not all bad or mad! She lost babies herself over the years, and I believe, that working on that 'evidence' it either proved that death happens, birth was precarious and it was all in the lap of the gods, or that, despite herself, Maggie may not have been as immune from the curse herself as she would have wished or wanted people to believe. Either way, I think that she believed herself to be at least aware of it. More in control of it. Able at least to realise that there was a risk and so it was 'safer' to insist on the children being under her stewardship, since this was the lesser of several evils. The other family members, who may or may not be contaminated, were unknown quantities, and for her, she worked on the principle, perhaps, that the devil you know, etc. She perhaps knew her own demons and could master them, whereas how could she be sure of other people's demons or their capacity to withstand them – particularly since she already had her doubts about Lena?

As for my own research into the family – this has been time consuming and not easy, but with time on my hands and an acknowledged maybe even unhealthy interest, I have made time, and great efforts to dig and delve. I found the right people to help me, using what contacts I have in all spheres of medicine, law and academia. I have not been at all shy in arm twisting and calling in favours; I have had to give many lectures in far-flung places, seen many clients without fee; reviewed favourably many books that – I have to admit - I was not all that struck on! -   in order to 'buy' people's expertise and cooperation.   But all this has been at least useful and productive.   The research has shed some light on the family background, and unsurprisingly – since there are probably no real 'true blue English people' left – no Anglos – let alone Anglo Saxons – their antecedents are more colourful and 'foreign' than they perhaps would have acknowledged!   Their background makes a mockery of their hostile and xenophobic attitude towards strangers. Having spent many hours with Gladys – and, as you will gather from my own words, having done what I could to research the matter -   I came to the conclusion that Maggie had definitely not just made the story up … or not in its entirety in any case. Her interpretation and memory of the things that had been passed on to her might be exaggerated or misremembered, factually, but the events and the crimes she spoke about COULD have taken place.   Neither do I believe that Gladys was in any way embroidering the facts.   If anything, I think she had given it a more 'Maggie might have been delirious' excuse in her own mind. I believe a bit of her was hoping that, though the story was the very one that she had been given, it was somehow just that, a story.   After all, how could one not be in denial of the terrible crimes and even more the inherited flaws, not just implied, but categorically advanced, about her own family, by her own mother on her deathbed!

I was concerned for Gladys' own mental health, but could just listen and hope for the best. I began to believe, too, that her visiting Helen, was her way of burying her own feelings, and in doing so trying to ensure that she was not part of history repeating itself, yet again.

Gladys did seem, genuinely, relieved that Susan was to all intents and purposes, much as she had ever been. She certainly did not seem to be all that adversely affected by the death of her mother, and neither did she seem to find the cause of her mother's death surprising or upsetting. To Gladys that was a good thing. To me, I was not sure that it was. To appear to take murder and revenge in her stride, seemed to me to fit the pattern of the Clement line all too well. There was nothing I could do, so I had to just try to keep a watching brief, albeit it from a distance, since, in truth, the 'case' was no longer anything to do with me. I would just be accused of the terrible professional crime – the cardinal sin of the social worker, or psychiatrist - of 'over-involvement' and worse, not just with a client, but now with an ex-client not to mention her entire family!

The Story below is my researched background to Maggie's story, with historical and explanatory inputs, gleaned from my delving into the archives of the various reference facilities available nowadays. In my retirement, I have been able to spend considerable amounts of time – and indeed money – on trying to ascertain the facts. Partly, of course, out of sheer curiosity, but also because it would be fascinating to know whether such a phenomenon as a 'perverse' or 'pernicious' gene really exists, and whether there are people who are born with such a handicap!

THE REAL HISTORY OF THE CLEMENT/COLLIER FAMILY

The family had, in fact, (so much for their hatred and mistrust of foreigners and snobs!) hailed originally from France. A French aristocrat had smuggled his two daughters across the channel to save them from the guillotine. They had sought refuge with a slight acquaintance of their father who had, in a moment of generosity, offered succour never believing that any of the family would be in a position to take him up on his offer. The two teenage girls, Marguerite, 15 and Helene, 14 had arrived out of the blue, with their elderly grandmother, to take up his offer. Their father and mother had both perished, as had a brother and his wife. The girls then, and the frail and elderly grandmother, were the only surviving members of the Clemenceau-DuPont family.

At a similar time, an Italian sailor, Francisco Martinelli, had jumped ship whilst moored in Bristol and had hidden himself away until the coast was clear. The ship had been bound for another long voyage to the East Indies and he was not in the mood for years more of hardship, floggings, storms, poor rations and scurvy which had been his life for too long, since he was 14. His mother had died when he was six, and his father had remarried – a widow, who already had five children of her own. The couple then had three more children, and though they were not cruel or neglectful of him, he had never really felt part of the now big and squabbling family. The family had lived their entire lives in Naples, so he had grown up with and around sailors and seafaring men. His father was from a fishing background, but had taken over an uncle's chandlery business on his death since he had no sons of his own. The family, then, were not really impoverished, though with so many mouths now to feed, there was certainly no great excess of wealth. It was, though, less the thought of poverty that had driven the boy away, so much as a need to see the world and to escape the familiarity of his confining surroundings. (*I apologise if this sounds a bit Hans Anderson - or perhaps the Brothers Grimm since there is no bed of roses, and certainly no crystal slipper that I can identify to save the family from themselves!).*

Anyway, Francisco returned into the port of Naples only twice since leaving. On his first return, he learned that his father had died trying to protect one of his stepsons. Apparently the young man, who was about 20, had got himself involved in an altercation over a young girl that he was trying to seduce, to which her father had naturally taken umbrage. The man had got between the boy and a punch which had made him topple, catching his foot on a hawser and hitting his head on the post which was retaining a fishing boat moored at anchor in the harbour. After this tragedy, his stepmother's eldest son had taken over the chandlery business, but by all accounts he had not been a good businessman, and had quickly lost heart and interest. The shop had been sold, for a pittance, and the woman had remarried an elderly farmer, who was glad to have company and several strong lads to help out on his land. There was no reason for Francisco to stay, and he saw no point in visiting any of his disparate family members.

On his second enforced visit to Naples, he remained out of sight, on board, until such time as they set sail again. So, more by default than design, he made his home in England – originally the West Country, but then moving gradually to London, gravitating towards a place that he considered would provide more opportunities.

Meanwhile, on the death of their grandmother, only three months after their arrival in England, the Clemenceau-Dupont girls were an encumbrance to their reluctant host and a nuisance to his wife and daughters. He succeeded in finding 'welcoming' homes for them in London. In today's terms, he probably could be said to have pimped them out to two of his passing and none too salubrious acquaintances. So it is safe to say that more was required of them to earn their keep than to be decorative and accomplished! Marguerite, the elder of the sisters, though she found the concept of being little more than a kept woman unattractive, nonetheless thought herself better off staying put – on the basis that better the devil you know! Her sister, Helene, not seeing herself as having been born and brought up to be an unpaid harlot, albeit a cocooned and well-dressed one, realised that once her looks and youth faded, she would likely be sent packing anyway, so preferred to take her chances while her strength and health would serve her better in finding another means of surviving and in the process keeping whatever earnings she made for her own benefit and not provide some 'dreary old coffin-dodger' with free entertainment!

So now both Francisco Martinelli and Helene Clemenceau-Dupont were both penniless and alone on the streets of London and seeking some way to earn a living. In the grand scheme of things, it was as lucky as not that they chanced to meet.

One bitterly cold night, Francisco came across Helene as she wrestled with a sailor outside a dockside tavern. It was not clear whether the sailor was trying to protect his money belt, or whether Helene was trying to protect her virtue, but Francisco decided that either way there was an opening for him. Whether out of avarice or amour-ice, Francisco jumped in to save Helene. Later she claimed that she was fighting off the unwelcome advances of the swarthy drunken sailor, fresh off a boat from the West Indies.

From what Francisco actually saw, he was more inclined to believe that her mind and hands were more set on his money-belt than fending the sailor off. Not being naïve or foolhardy, however, at no time, then or after, did he ever say as much to his potential new source of revenue, sex and partnership! In actual fact, he was only half right! Helen had long since decided that food held a higher priority than virtue but she was determined not to be cheated out of her rightful earnings by the sailor who had agreed a price but was trying to renege! Motivation notwithstanding, Francisco was the very epitome of chivalry and bravery, not only chasing away the sailor – who was extremely unsteady on his legs, so easy-pickings for the lightweight, but nimble, young man, but insisting on comforting her with a drink in a nearby hostelry – yes, of course, with the sailor's – and perhaps Helene's, hard earned coppers!

The duo did not so much fall in love, as fall into 'business', each providing convenience, security, opportunities and companionship for one another.   To neither was it the love of their lives.   Neither had any real need for, or expectation of, such a fanciful and impractical concept, but each found it comforting to not be alone, to have somebody to share the hardships, the hustle for money to survive, and some warmth during cold and hungry nights.

Despite the facts that we already know, the story Francisco told, when first he met Helene Clemenceau-Dupont (who by that time was calling herself – for professional reasons, one supposes, Nell Clements!) was that he had no idea who his father had been, but his mother had allegedly descended from well-to-do stock.   She had fallen hook line and sinker for a ne'er do well English so-called gentleman who was taking part in a grand tour of Europe.   This infatuation on his part and profound love on hers, was apparently short lived, with him moving on to other sights to see, people to meet. She faced abandonment, ostracisation and ruin.

Francisco was - according to his flowery regaling of this fairytale renaissance to all his new acquaintances, including Helene - the consequence of this short lived liaison, and so he was now, as he saw it, in the land of his father – whose name he barely knew, and certainly did not share, and who he would not recognise even should he pass him as he walked penniless along the wealthy parts of the city of London. *(From what I could discover, he was nothing if not a schmaltzer!)*

Francisco Martinelli now calling himself Francis Martins, and Helene Clemenceau-Dupont, now Nell Clements, never married – neither each other nor anybody else – until their deaths. From an Italian sailor and a French aristocrat, now no better than beggars, the Clement dynasty was born in the back alleys and dingy streets of the heaving, fetid and diverse city of London - a city where the rich were very rich and the poor were very poor, and neither side had any sympathy nor respect for the other.

The couple lived in many of the poorer areas of the East End of London, always failing to pay their rent, and only staying until neighbours became too fed up with them cadging from them. They were both very charming when things were going well, but became argumentative and threatening – both to one another, and to everybody else in the vicinity – when, as was often, life was not so easy.

Nell died very young, aged 27, giving birth to their fifth child *(though I could only find evidence of only two previous infants – girls - surviving past the first weeks of infancy and both of those were abandoned by Nell and consequently brought up in the local workhouse).* With this fifth baby, a neighbour, Anne Goodrich, had been called upon to assist in the birth which was not going well. She had sent Francis out to try and fetch one of the birthing women (an older woman better used to difficult births and miscarriages) but he had not done this and had gone to the public house instead. When Anne Goodrich found him to tell him that Nell had not survived but that his daughter was healthy and he should come, he knew he was neither able nor willing to look after the tiny baby. He had had precious little to do with the previous unfortunate infants, and he had no real desire to do so now, particularly on his own. Nell was dead. She was of no further use to him nor him to her. It was time to make himself scarce. He never returned to the house, and simply disappeared into the night and was never seen again.

The baby miraculously survived and was taken in by Anne who, despite living in equally poor and squalid conditions with four other children, had sufficient Christian charity to not see the baby die in the gutter. She called her Helen, since that had been her mother's name, but the child was never Christened, and not even registered as a birth until many years later when the neighbour also died. It then became necessary for all the children, Anne's own – of which only two were alive by then - and Helen, to be taken to the local Workhouse. Helen, then 7, was able to give them details of her name and date of birth, as she had learned them from her foster-mother. This information was only too easily corroborated by local people since Francis and Nell had been somewhat notorious and their sins and transgressions were only too well known to all and sundry. Her mother's name was registered as Helen Clement, AKA Nell Clement, but it was not possible to register a father since Francis was not around in order to confirm this and in any case, Nell's line of work made it perhaps a leap of faith too far to ascribe a father for the child. Though it was neither acknowledged by any of them, though it was most certainly known to the authorities, she was then living under the same roof as at least two of her sisters *(I say 'at least', because with Helen's lifestyle and lack of any attempt on her part to formally register or record any – indeed any - of her births –*

either dead or alive - she may well have had other babies that she had abandoned and who may or may not have ended up in that workhouse as well). Naturally, though I obviously did not actually know that particular Helen - Helen Clement - I feel confident to guess, that the fact that she had siblings there would have meant absolutely nothing to her – indeed they may well have been in mortal danger if she had known. On the other hand, if Maggie's gene theory is sound, she too might have been in equal danger!

One fact that was also the gossip of the neighbourhood, after Anne Goodrich's death, was speculation about the unfortunate circumstances surrounding the death of her last baby when he was four days old. Although it had been seen as a blessing in disguise by everybody else, Anne had been devastated. The baby had died during the night, and Anne went to her death believing that she had rolled over and accidentally smothered him. From the gossip around, following her death, and the removal of Helen to the Workhouse the rumour-mill was rife with the story – told by Anne's surviving eldest son - that young Helen had actually told playmates that it was her. Helen had repaid her foster-mother by smothering her youngest baby when it was four days old, because she resented his young presence. In particular, she took umbrage at the fact that he had usurped her place next to her 'mother' in the bed, which she had previously held as the youngest child. Helen was four years old at the time. The pattern had begun!

(Note from me. *One would have to wonder, though, about the deaths of Helen's siblings who had died in the care of her now dead mother, Helene (Nell). Who can say whether poor conditions, lack of food, lack of care, natural weakness, or a hand or pillow over the mouth brought about their journeys to heaven!*)

Though Helen Clement had been too young to remembered him, since the early years when she had heard the story in all its graphic detail, she vowed never to forgive her father Francis, and this antipathy towards men remained with her throughout her entire life. She was eventually hanged for the stabbing of a stall holder in a London market when he caught her stealing a turkey, which she had hoped to sell for the price of many a tankard of ale.

Long before that, though, Francis had finally been forced back to sea, fearing for his life since he had pickpocketed an individual who was not as vulnerable as he had thought. He escaped from London with his life, but since the man had many allies and spies in London, Francis took the only option that he considered possible, and ran, first to the east coast, via Colchester, then on to Harwich, where he took work on the first ship that presented itself. His new ship - a major cargo-carrying vessel operating over long distances between Europe and the Far East - was crewed by much harder and less forgiving men than he had sailed with previously. After many months at sea, at their first port of call, Francis – now reverting to Francisco – got extremely drunk, tried to steal tobacco from the pocket of a local dockworker, and got subjected to a thorough beating. On his way back to the ship, walking unsteadily, he tripped on the dockside, and toppled, unseen, into the sea between the boats.

There is a bit of a gap in my census information, because as you can guess the surviving Clement girls were not easy to track once they left the Workhouse. Even after I picked up the trail, it proved a challenge because they were fairly nomadic and unable or unwilling to comply with any kind of requirement to register for anything or anyone. For whatever reason, I was unable to pick up the family again on record until the period best covered by Maggie's story. The information I gathered, however, did go some way to back-up the dubious nature of the Clement tradition.

But, all that is, as they say, 'history' is it not? The sins of the fathers – or mothers in this case – surely cannot be visited on their offspring, and on generations to come. I know there is a line of thought that believes such a harsh gospel, but I have seen – thankfully – little sign of it in my work, or in my life.

There was, however, one very important liaison that Maggie never mentioned at all to Gladys, let alone elaborated on. Whether she left it out of the story because it vexed her, or whether it simply embarrassed her, I cannot say. I have discussed it with Gladys since, and, showing just how much circumstances – and I suppose time – has changed her, she finds it simultaneously both sad and funny! From my own researches, I discovered that in the mid 1880's, Gladys's grandmother, also Margaret, but known as Peggy, lived, surrounded by relatives in Shoreditch in east London. When she was 17, still young and unmarried, she had followed in her French ancestor's footsteps and met and fallen for the charms of a foreign sailor. This, though, was not an Italian sailor but a Russian sailor, whose familial name was Abelev, Leonid Abelev. Very soon after arriving in England, Leonid had Anglicised his name to Leonard Able, but his parents and their parents, and their parents before them, had all been orthodox Jews, though Leonard no longer practiced, nor indeed advertised, his faith nor his antecedents. Whether this was because he was disillusioned with his religion or whether he was fearful of discrimination or being alien, it is impossible to say. If he was actually hostile to his previous faith, or hostile to his antecedents, then his views could have influenced Peggy, then and forever more. More likely, though, it was his subsequent abandonment of her, when she was pregnant with Maggie, that was a more potent factor. In truth, only she could probably say, but the hatred had certainly transmitted itself down to her daughter, and thence on to her granddaughters, thereafter. Whether it was a solidarity with Leonard, or a hatred of Leonard, seems somewhat irrelevant, since either one or both were responsible for their collective attitude towards 'foreigners', 'interlopers' and 'Jewboys'!

Gladys was definitely somewhat surprised then to learn that her mother was Jewish, and that she came from a long line of Jewish people, and Russians at that! It was even stranger now to be having such a long overdue conversation, after all those years, since we were now unfortunately heading hell for leather for the thick of the 'cold war' when the villain of the piece was undoubtedly the Russians, and when many people thought the 'Ruskies' would blow us all up at any moment. It was perhaps not such a good time to find out that one was a Russian! Maggie would have been less than delighted to have it announced that she was not only second generation Jewish, but that her father was Russian! She obviously did know, but for her to know was one thing, for the world at large to know, was quite another.

Chapter 19:   Susan's Story

I had seen her watching us.   At first I was not sure whether I was imagining things, but then she was there so often that it seemed that it had to be true.   Sometimes she wore a school uniform, sometimes she was dressed in dreadful – and I mean dreadful – jack up jeans – like her trousers had had a row with her ankles - and a really dire jumper ... with bloody Bambi on it, for goodness sake!   She even wore her icky school lace-ups with the jeans!   How awful is that!

I don't know how I knew who she was – well I didn't for a while – but then one day I was looking through Nan's old photograph album, and something about the shape of the face – I don't know – I like a draw and like life drawing best – no, not just because they are naked! – I am good at seeing, really seeing, people – ears, eyes – how close they are together, all kinds of things that sometimes other people don't see so well.   Anyway, for whatever reason, I just knew it was her.   I had never seen her, but I just knew it was her.... I just knew.   Nobody could have been more surprised than me that morning when she turned up at the house.   I had no idea who Beatrice – my mum – was chatting with out of the window – so when she walked in the room, well ... I nearly choked on my toast!

I had seen her the day I lost my purse – she was practically in my pocket when I bought the bleedin' ticket, but it had become a bit of a laugh by then.   God alone knows what she thought she was doing – but she must have been sorry 'cos we ended up climbing up all those effing stairs – AGAIN!   I really thought, though, that I had just lost the wallet – I'll give her that, she must have been quick as anything, cos I never felt or sensed her take it!   I somehow knew, when she brought it back, that it wasn't just a social visit – but she was so … sort of 'normal', even though, somehow I just knew what she was going to do.   I guess I would have done the exact same thing!   But I couldn't stick around just the same – that would have been … well, it would have been too weird!   So I left.   I didn't really know Beatrice, and I can't say I liked her much.   She even expected me to call her Mum – what a bloody joke! There was absolutely no way that I was going to ride to the rescue!   I'm not kinky enough to want to stick around and watch, and, to be honest, I thought there was a chance that Nan might spoil the party – so I made a strategic retreat. That way, I neither had to help nor hinder! If I had to choose, then, I guess I would have been more likely to help than to hinder!   I guess that might sound gruesome, but I find I have a fairly high tolerance for gruesome.   From eavesdropping on Aggie Maggie's conversation with Nan – I was young, but as they say "little pigs have big ears!" - before she popped her clogs, I should think I must be a typical Barber. I gather murder runs in the family. BUT ... unlike the useless versions of recent times, I should warn everyone, that should I go in for homicide, like my older and obviously cleverer ancestors, I have absolutely no intention of getting found out. There's nothing clever about spending your life behind bars! I have not found anybody I want to bump off yet, but then I am still young and who knows what the future may hold.

It is quite possible that even from miles away Maeve might have had burning ears or a crisis of confidence at this self-diagnosis on the part of Susan! And to be honest I was less than sanguine myself! Eamonn, one of the Clarkin boys, now men, I suppose, was mid-way through a Master's Degree in Social Policy at Loughborough. His field of study – don't blame me, I had nothing to do with it – was the Law and Mental Competence, and since he had virtually been brought up with one of the most enigmatic and complex examples of this, with the enthusiastic agreement of Helen, he was allowed to visit her and 'interview' both her and me. That was perfectly fine, except that on the day that had been arranged for the visit (and I was doing the chauffeuring!) he arrived somewhat early and I had an unexpected – and rare – call at my house from Susan. She had got some sketches which she wanted Helen to have – sketches made from photographs of Elizabeth, Helen's mother, which she had found in the photograph album.   I thought it was very thoughtful of her, but had learned to be wary of Susan, since she was not always saying what she meant and her thought processes could be decidedly complicated.   Though I tried to steer Mon (as Eamonn was more usually called) in a different direction, but to no avail.   Nothing draws two people together – not just young people, though they are more susceptible -   quicker than being warned off one another – so the inevitable happened and the two were immediately 'an item'. Had I been a true scholar, or a person who thought it was interesting to pull the wings off of butterflies to see if they could still fly, I might have been absolutely intrigued to sit, glasses on, notebook at the ready, pencil poised, to record the outcome of such an experiment!   But if I ever was that person, I am certainly not her now!   So I was, to say the least, 'concerned'.   If I had been Gladys, I would have put it more bluntly, I would have been 'shitting bricks'!

PART FIVE

Chapter 20:   Moving gingerly forward!

It is true to say that I was getting too old to do much more than hold a kind of watching brief – physically I found it tiring, but I have to say that mentally I was still intrigued and fascinated by it all.   I often wondered whether the whole thing was smoking mirrors and whether Maggie was up there – or I suppose down there! – somewhere having a good laugh at my expense.

Helen had been locked away for getting on for half her lifetime for avenging her mother – almost longer now than her victim had served for despatching Elizabeth, ostensibly over a fur coat, but really, I would suggest, as a result of sheer prejudice and bad blood.   I am not using the term 'bad blood' in the sense that we might interpret Maggie's fears, but in the more common or garden sense of prejudice and resentment.   Nothing special about that – most murders that are committed, that are not robbery related, have a big element of either one or both of those triggers.   I was getting fairly complacent and beginning to relax and believe that the whole notion of an inherited 'murder' gene had been Maggie's manufacture and my own gullibility.

I was still in touch sporadically with Gladys and had, at her request, gone with her to Lena's funeral, which was held in Essex, Canvey Island, in fact, where she had gone to live towards the end of her life. According to Gladys 'she had a good innings' but a very sad end.

She had left London partly because of her falling out with her mother, but also because she had begun to suffer very much from chest problems. To quote Gladys, she had the cough of a coalman! The air out of London seemed to have done her some good, because she seemed to pick up and feel better; she lost a bit of weight (which, again according to Gladys!) was not a moment too soon and 'the silly cow could have put up a better fight against the fags if she had not been so idle!'. By the sea she had been living a much more active life and so had felt much less lethargic and hence happier in herself. Eventually though she had suffered a series of mini-strokes which had made her sometimes confused, frightened and vulnerable. This had a masking effect because it disguised the fact that she had indeed been suffering for some time from lung cancer – the symptoms of which she had studiously ignored out of fear and the ostrich effect. This had developed secondaries, or in medical speak, it had metastasised in her brain. She had died alone in hospital, aged 64. She had had relatively little contact with the London family over the years, sending Christmas and birthday cards, sometimes with a note of news, frequently just signed, which was apparently reciprocated by her sisters. On a couple of occasions, when they had the time, and when they felt like a trip to the seaside the sisters had individually trekked down to Canvey island. Neither had stayed with Lena during their time there, but rented chalets and merely visited on an occasion or two, spending such time as seemed appropriate but certainly not making it their primary motive for being there. Though they were cordial and pleasant to one another, their meetings could never be described as affectionate or sisterly. Too much water had flowed under too many bridges, and there were too many shared memories which they would all much rather forget. Most people would have seen this as 'sad', but from Gladys, and from my brief – very brief – conversations with Connie, I gathered that both of them were more comfortable with the separation and though it would have been disrespectful to not attend the funeral – and would have reflected badly on the family – over the intervening years, there had been no real desire on anybody's part to hold out a real hand of friendship, let alone re-establish the previous closeness.

They were all quite happy with their lives. To an observant outsider, their relationships with anybody/everybody could best be described as 'distant' and 'practical'. Even Gladys' constant – and to the outside world exemplary – dedication to visiting and championing Helen, was really a need to live up to her charge as 'head' of the family, and to continue to make amends, on behalf of the family, for what had been a moment of madness by her daughter, Beattie ..." the silly bitch, not an 'apporth of sense nor reason, silly cow" …. (To quote Gladys on more than one occasion, or words of similar meaning and sense).

As for Connie, I am less familiar with her and even less conversant with her current circumstances. I gather she separated – not divorced, I don't think – from her poor benighted husband who was probably quite relieved to have gained his freedom from the whole family. She had now, apparently, settled down with a 'Gyppo' – (once again to quote Gladys!). I have interpreted this as the fact that he is a showman – working for a carnival – but I could be wrong. He might actually BE a Gypsy – a Romany, perhaps from Eastern Europe, or a Traveller from Ireland … who can say! Either way, the whole concept is both comforting and surprising. From a family steeped in prejudice and hatred of 'them bleedin' foreigners', as long as the poor man survives 'the gene' I'd see that as a step in the right direction. But that could just be me trying to shape the world to my preferences.

I have less knowledge of any of the 'children' who are, of course, children no longer. Connie does not seem to talk about any of them, so I just don't know whether they are all living with Connie and the new man in her life, or whether they have all gone their separate ways. I am assuming that they are all alive and well, but I would be more comfortable knowing that none of them were now themselves mothers ... in particular mothers of daughters. I know that I have often expressed my scepticism over the 'gene', but discretion being the better part of valour, I would rather err on the side of caution, and would certainly either prescribe 'the pill' for them all, or have them all sterilised! That might seem very harsh, given that it would be to say the least precautionary, with the jury still out on the 'gene' theory, but I won't be around for ever to keep a watching brief on the Barber dynasty!

Chapter 21.   No peace for the wicked!

After many months – nearly three years in fact, but in retirement time has only a notional importance in my life.   It is not that I don't do anything – I am certainly not 'just a lady who knits!' but the things I do no longer have any kind of 'delivery' element: I do them when I want, and don't do them when I don't want!   I would have seen it as somewhat wasteful and indulgent before but now I find it extremely pleasant and wish I had been more 'laid back' over the years!

Anyway, back to the story … Out of the blue I had a very late night call from Maeve.   We had kept in touch in a superficial way – postcards from holidays, birthdays, Christmas, that kind of thing – and I had once, early on, gone over to stay for a few days because I was attending a Conference in Cork University.   *It would have been unfriendly and ungrateful (given her support of Helen) not to have visited.   I had been persuaded to extend my stay past the conference dates, and had enjoyed my time with them very much.*

Maeve asked if it was at all possible for me to put up Kevin for a couple of nights.   She was stuck at home because they had a full house most nights in the Guest House (which had now grown virtually into a proper hotel!) and also the restaurant, which had in recent years got very pleasing reviews in the Good Food Guide, so was very busy too. Although her eldest son, Connor, was to all intents and purposes running the place now, she and Kevin were reluctant to just abandon him and both take off at the same time.

I said, of course. I did not ask why he was coming over, since that might sound like I was hesitant about saying yes or being too nosy. I would have hated for her to think I needed an explanation rather than just offering hospitality without strings.

Kevin arrived hot foot from Euston the next day, looking, I have to say, only slightly older than I had remembered him all those years ago. The trip across on the boat, followed by the boat-train was never a relaxing one – not spoken from experience, I should add, but I have often heard tell. I had the benefit of being funded to travel over, so had flown (*not so common at the time and most 'ordinary' people seemed to think primarily in terms of the boat!*). The Irish sea is one of the roughest crossings so he was probably not at his best. After the pleasantries and me showing him to his room, and putting the kettle on, he asked if I had a train timetable, or if he could please use my telephone. I told him that unfortunately I did not have a train timetable, but that he was welcome to use the telephone any time and to make the house his home for so long as he was there. He seemed very friendly, but slightly on edge, but since I did not know him well, I assumed it could be because his wife had made the arrangement with me, and he would much have preferred to book into a hotel or stay with one of the kids. I somehow assumed that one or more of them might be either permanently or temporarily living in London – since all of them had been born in the city, and it was their home town, even if their parents had hailed from elsewhere and had returned to Ireland. A lot of them had originally gone over, of course, because they were all young enough for that to be sensible, but I also knew – from my visit there – that they were mostly all now free agents, and were scattered and far-flung. I guess it was a bit of an assumption that one or more of them was back here, in London, but I thought the odds were probably good. Anyway, that was my thinking – completely wrong as it happened! I should have realised that for the young nowadays the world has completely shrunk and the globe is just a backpack away! They were in fact scattered to the four corners – like their ancestors before them!

I had not even had any contact with Mon for ages, and I had been surprised that he had not contacted me at the end of his Masters, which I presumed he had gained with flying colours. I did not want thanks or any kind of acknowledgement, but I was interested and anxious to know that it had gone well for him and what he was doing now – since he was to some extent working in my own field of expertise. I find it awful now to add that I had not once, in over three years, ever given a thought to Susan, much less what I had assumed would be her passing fling with Mon.

I had continued to visit Helen, and had seen Gladys once or twice in passing, or when she wanted me to take something up to her niece. She was in poor health and sometimes no longer able to do the journey herself. I have to say, I am not that much younger, but I have the benefit of having always been a single lady without children, and able to be selfish enough to spend my money on driving lessons and car purchase, otherwise I might have been more handicapped myself. I am not getting any younger either.

Kevin said if it was all right with me, could he stay that one night, then he needed to make a trip, and if he could return then to stay prior to catching the boat train back, that would be wonderful. I said whatever he needed. I did not want to pry, but really thought that if he could tell me where he needed to go, I might be better able to help him and feel more useful. But it seemed to me that there was some kind of problem, and a problem that he was both worried about but anxious to play down. I could not force him to confide if he preferred not to.

Early the next morning, he set off for the train station, still not really saying where he was going, or why. Short of asking him outright, I was not in a position to do or say anything. I had to just mind my own business, and say I would see him when he returned. He said he would ring and let me know, but I gave him a key and said he could if it was convenient, but if he had the key, he could just come and go as he pleased. I was not one at that time for going too far afield, but neither did I want to just sit by the telephone waiting to let him in if and when he returned.

Much later that night, about half eleven, I was in bed but reading, when the telephone rang. I assumed it was Kevin, and to tell the truth was somewhat miffed. He had a key so he could just come if he was coming; if he wasn't he did not have to ring all! I was surprised, then, to hear Maeve's voice. She apologised for the lateness of the hour, but said they had only just closed the restaurant and she had been rushed off her feet. I said it was all right, but if she wanted to speak to Kevin, he was not here, and had gone off early morning, and would return when he returned. I explained I had given him a key and told him to come and go as he pleased.

Maeve went quite silent, and I began to wonder if the two of them had had a falling out, and if Kevin had, in fact, left her. I reminded myself how silly a suggestion that was, since it was Maeve herself who had made the arrangement with me on his behalf. Eventually she spoke again.

"Eddie" she said, "I think we are in trouble! None of us have heard from Mon for ages and he was a little gobshite frequently, but never hurtful and never went this long without letting us know that he was all right."

I said, "He's probably travelling – some places are not that easy to phone out of – and he is not one, I don't think, for Wish you were Here postcards!"

"I thought of that, but when I spoke to Susan, she was cagey, wouldn't give me a straight answer. I know she was not my number one fan, but we have always been straight with one another. She told me I was an interfering old bugger, and I told her she was a bullying, callous and ill-mannered bastard, but neither one of us hedged or pussy-footed around. Mother-in-Law/Daughter-in-Law syndrome, I suppose."

That took me by surprise. I had never imagined – in my wildest dreams – that Mon and Susan would still be part of one another's lives, let alone a married couple.

"God, Maeve, I did not know they had got married. I knew they were seeing a bit of one another – they met here actually, I must admit. But they were both young, busy and with their whole lives ahead of them, I imagined it would be a five-minute wonder."

"No, not married, as such! Just my exaggerating. But Susan felt like my daughter-in-law. But, oh, God, how I wish it had been a five-minute wonder! They have had absolute murders over the years – you cannot imagine!"

I can, I thought! But the very idea of using Susan and murder in the same sentence sent shivers down my spine. I know that Maeve obviously knew about Helen, but as far as I know, nobody had told her about 'the gene'. I realised that to her 'murder' was a figure of speech – not a description of what, heaven forbid, had befallen her lovely son since he may well be married – if not in law at least in danger - to the latest in a long line of sociopaths – maybe even psychopaths. Was it helpful to tell her? I thought not, for the time being, though that decision could come back to haunt me. But for now, since there was nothing she could do over there except worry, I considered it kinder and more practical to say nothing.

"Maeve, do you know where they were living? Is that where Kevin has gone, do you think?"

"I'm almost sure he will start there – unless he has managed to get hold of one or other of them on the phone beforehand. They were living in Nottingham – Mon got a job at the university after he finished his Masters...... Somewhere near a place called Southwich, I think. Susan was working too – for a vet, I think, though she was always falling out and either getting fired, or leaving. She is like a firecracker – goes off the deep end for everything and nothing."

The thought of Susan being around a drugs cupboard and being volatile, sent shivers down my spine, but I had to stay reasonably non-committal in case Maeve picked up on my agitation and it made matters worse. I was only too well aware how much worse matters could actually get. But no point in getting ahead of myself.

Kevin obviously did not return that night. Since he had a key anyway and would not be locked out, I could not resist my natural and life-long urge to do something rather than nothing. I decided very early the next morning to drive up to the address that Maeve had given me the night before. I had promised her that I would keep her in the picture and that I would try and keep Kevin safe and out of harm, if I could. She had no idea how empty a promise that might be, since she had no idea how deadly the situation actually was. I did believe, however, that the one that was most in danger – if he had not fallen foul of the 'gene' already - was Mon. I believed that, if the presence of the 'gene' was fact and not myth, that Kevin's sheer size and the surprise of him turning up would save him. If Susan had found some reason to want to be done with Mon, she would have planned it, even if she was angry, she would still have had the presence of mind, the inner cunning, the collective and inherited experience, if you like, to not act impulsively. I had to admit that my very agitation, and the almost acknowledged acceptance of my own fears at that point seemed to argue that even I had somehow accepted the possibility. And that, despite every bone in my body and brain in my head telling me that it was impossible, improbable, absolute rubbish!

I got into my car and headed north. As I drove, I realised, of course, that my logic over the safety of Kevin was groundless, since Susan's own mother had, in fact, killed absolutely on the spur of the moment. Yes, of course, she acted as the result of an established and systematic indoctrination from the family of Elizabeth's failings and her very intrusion into their tight and insular circle, but ultimately, the actual murder had been spontaneous and spur of the moment. That could happen, could it not, with Kevin too? I drove that much faster, all the time veering from thinking how silly I was being, what a stupid notion to believe that any of that was possible, to how silly I was to think that I could do anything to save anybody, to how silly I was to believe I could be a greater match for a born murderer than a 5ft 11in, knocking on a bit, but still well-built and burly fellow like Kevin, let alone a 6ft 2in youthful, intelligent and athletic young man like Mon.

Even if murder was/had been intended, I tried to convince myself, as I drove, Susan would not, could not succeed. Unlike her predecessors, surely she was not dealing with babies, weaklings, unsuspecting and vulnerable innocents. Surely Elizabeth had only been a victim because she had been taken completely by surprise – and how could she have anticipated such an outcome? What sane person would expect such a reaction over a family disagreement, however much the resentment had been obvious for years. Ordinary people, ordinary family members, just did not murder one another over fur coats, or petty jealousies – not even full-grown prejudices ... normally, anyway! That I saw as the fly in the ointment – the wrong equation in my previous thinking when I persuaded myself that Kevin, and/or Mon would be safe, because of Susan's very devious and organised thought processes. What if Mon, or Kevin, or both had, like Elizabeth, been taken by surprise. That would, to some extent, be my fault, would it not? I had known the possibility – was it a probability? – for years, and I had said absolutely nothing. I had stood by and personally watched as a relationship was established – at the very moment that they met and the spark was lit – knowing that it was/at least could be an accident waiting to happen! Worse, of course, was the fact that it would not be an 'accident' would it! It would/could be the end of two lives – and now maybe more – who could have predicted …. That was the horrifying, nagging, thought ... I, me, I could have predicted! I had done nothing, warned nobody, gone on with my safe and secure life, my selfish and comfortable retirement and given absolutely no real thought to the consequences. I just went on visiting Helen, listening to Gladys vaguely talk about Susan having moved 'up north' and not even bothered to worry about who she had 'moved up north' with …. it did not matter, did it, because I had no responsibility for a stranger, no obligation to anybody – somebody I did not know, somebody I had no interest in. And all along, it had been Mon she had 'gone up north' with; a lad I had watched growing, talked with, talked about. I'd concerned myself with his studies – with our shared interest – but all the time it was his very life that I could have saved. Helen would never forgive me! Of all the people in the world, almost without exception, even James possibly, Maeve and Kevin were the dearest people to her heart. They had been part of the Helen story since her very birth; Maeve who had been the best friend that any person could have had, who had not only found Elizabeth, James and Helen their very first family home, but had picked up the pieces when calamity had struck. Had been much more than a surrogate mother to Helen, a rock for James, a matchmaker in his meeting and marrying Sofia, a help to Sofia with their precious gift of the twins. It just did not bear thinking about. And now, through my thoughtlessness, her own precious son might be in danger of his life. Since I had now gone into a more negative and foreboding state as I drove along the relatively newly opened M1, with its endless straightness, I convinced myself that it was worse than that, Mon was already dead, and Kevin was walking into a situation he had no preparation for. So, devoid of anything to keep my interest apart from pointing the car northwards, I was soon wallowing in my own maudlin and fatalistic thoughts.

By the time I had to leave the motorway and concentrate on the more intricate driving on the 'ordinary' roads, I was calmer – thankfully not 'resigned' to calamity, but actively picking through my brain for more positive facets of the whole debacle. The thing that began to sustain me, was the realisation that, like me, Mon should have become better schooled than most in 'seeing' a psychopath. Surely if you live with somebody who is mentally unstable, and have an expertise in that subject, you must be better protected? Surely! Surely knowledge is power! He was not an unsuspecting and completely vulnerable hostage to fortune then.

I also began to rationalise the whole situation. Susan herself had a perfect knowledge of the 'family curse', having eavesdropped on Maggie's dying orders to Gladys. She had been young at the time, but, when we spoke, she had seemed extraordinarily blasé and matter of fact about the whole thing! It had been quite difficult to judge – even for a trained pair or ears like mine – whether she was being flippant because she was frightened, because she was disbelieving, or because she was excited and accepting of the bizarre notion. Whichever way, surely over several years living together, she must have confided in Mon – it must have come up in conversation, mustn't it? Was it possible that she lived with him and said nothing? She had seemed quite a forthright girl – young woman – and not a shrinking violet type, so … I guess it depended upon whether she had any capacity to have true feelings for him or not.

The family history would not give one a lot of confidence in her forming a proper, trusting, honest relationship with men, but perhaps with the 'right' man, that might be different?   I had to hope. I had to hope that she would be either sufficiently besotted, or sufficiently wary of her own capabilities and propensities, to be on her guard. She might have told him. She could have told him in a fit of pique, or in a moment of tenderness and distress, or because she thought she needed his help.   She might have told him, might she not? Possibly, but equally though she might have decided to – what was that saying – 'keep her powder dry' knowing that as a last resort if he was leaving her, or he upset her in some way, or she just got fed up with him, she had murder in her locker.   She had already implied – boasting or in jest, I would not like now to give a definitive verdict – that she felt she was not only well up for the family business, but would be better than any of them at it! Definitely when she had spoken, it seemed to me that she was almost in thrall to the 'gene' notion.   But she was a bit of an attention seeker, I thought –   even according to her grandmother, and Helen – so maybe it was all talk, all bravado.   I had to hope for one of those choices; either it was all bravado, or she had confided in Mon, and he was well prepared.   But where the hell was he?   Why did Susan just not say to Maeve "He's gone to Timbuctoo", or "We've gone our separate ways, and he has moved to Glasgow" ……

anything, rather than just hedge and prevaricate! And if either of those scenarios is the right one, why has Mon himself not contacted his mother to let her know where he is, and that he is all right?

I just drove on, almost reaching my destination, completely unable to plan what to do when I got there. What did one say, turning up on somebody's doorstep "Have you killed your boyfriend?" "Are you the next link in the chain?"

Chapter 22:   At least somebody's happy

Maeve was worried sick.   There had been no news of Kevin for twenty-four hours, and Eddie had told her that he had set off for Nottingham.   Surely if he had found Mon he would have rung by now – no news was definitely not good news.   He would have found the nearest telephone box and rung her – she knew that.   So, it was clear then, that either he had not found Mon, or what he found was not good news.   She was obviously not expecting murderous news – because she was unaware of the background – but she was fearful of more 'normal', and just as disastrous news, because she was a mother and she always worried, regardless.   Surely if he was in a road a traffic accident – he was always risking life and limb cycling around all that traffic! – she would have heard, Susan would have said!   It was one thing to cycle around here – the wilds of County Cork – but …   Maeve had lived in England, London in fact, for many years, and she well remembered how precarious it was to run the gauntlet as a pedestrian, let alone sharing the roads with the big lorries and the boy racers!   Or he could be seriously ill!   A brain tumour!   A heart attack!   Young people do have heart attacks, young Seamus Donovan had one only last year, and he was only 23!   Why would Kevin not ring!

Though Connor was now the principal proprietor of the hotel – and had overseen all of the expansion and the growth – normally his wife, Siobhan, would have been his mainstay doing the admin and the day to day management of the staff. She was recuperating at the moment, however, because she had just given birth to their first baby, and though mother and baby were now well, it had not been an easy birth. Unlike all of Maeve's 8 confinements which had, as Kevin often said, "gone like shelling peas!", Cecilia, their latest granddaughter, weighing just 4lbs 2oz, had been born by Caesarean section and Siobhan had almost lost her life. She was, naturally, taking time to recuperate and get herself well again. Maeve was needed now to help Connor, and also to try to support her daughter-in-law who was not finding first time motherhood easy, especially since she did not feel very fit herself. Kevin, surprisingly, though having been a wonderful father and husband over the years, had probably been spoiled by having a wife that coped easily with anything that life and nature threw at her, and to Maeve's surprise, and Connor's annoyance, had been less than patient with his 'prima donna' daughter-in-law! It had been an easy decision to send Kevin to England in search of Mon, rather than Maeve going herself – despite the fact that Kevin himself was seriously ill at the present time, with the early stages of pancreatic cancer. He had been receiving some treatment for it, but by and large, it was needing to take its course, and they had resigned themselves to the fact that he only had a short time left to him. Maeve was putting a brave face on it, and up to that point they had not told any of the children – not even Connor, who was becoming critical of his father's lack of patience and his increasing slowness and lack of support with the heavier work around the hotel. Maeve was in two minds. Kevin had forbidden her from saying anything, wanting everybody to treat him as normal, but Maeve knew that when the time came – and soon – when it became common knowledge, either because he became so ill, or he died, that Connor would be mortified that he had given him such a hard time, and had been so disparaging. He would blame Maeve, and it would sour their relationship too. But she had promised Kevin, so she was duty bound to honour her promise. Whatever the consequences.

So in Kevin and Siobhan's absence she was in great demand at the hotel. It was not easy to have to run the front of house of an hotel and restaurant business as well as worry about all kinds of things – husbands, sons, daughters-in-law, granddaughters - but with good staff and a laid back and easy going clientele, things continued to tick over.

The morning after her conversation with Maeve and still with no word from Kevin, she was in the hotel office, pretending to be checking invoices but really just praying and calling on the goodwill of every and any saint she had ever read about, when the phone rang on the desk – an internal call – and she was tempted to not answer it. What could they want her for now.   Nothing was important enough to merit her time just now!   But it kept on ringing, and she kept on ignoring it.   Suddenly the office door opened, and Grainne, normally the bane of her life, and possibly the most endearing, but least competent receptionist that Ireland had ever produced, put her head around the door and said "Did ye not hear that ringing – and it's right by your head!   You're wanted!"

"Shut up, Graw, and go back to your work – whatever it is, you will have to sort it.   I'm busy, and don't have time right now!"

"I think you might have time for this, though, Mrs. Clarkin …. I think you might have time – defferably – for this!"

Maeve knew that either something was seriously wrong or something really mad had happened since none of the staff were expected – or encouraged – to call her or Kevin, Mr. or Mrs Clarkin. They were always Maeve and Kevin.   There was no real hierarchy or top table in their world – though it was an efficiently and well run world – efficient, but democratic!

Sighing, she got up and picking up her cardigan which was slung over the back of the chair and putting it around her shoulders, she went around the desk and followed in the retreating footsteps of Grainne.

The sight that awaited her made her burst into tears on the spot – much to her son's surprise. There stood Mon, with several days' growth of beard, rucksack slung over his back, and a jumper tied around his waist.

"God Almighty, why the tears! What in God's name's wrong with you? Are you not pleased to see me – I'll go if not – I can always push off to stay with Colette!"

"Don't you dare go anywhere! Where have you been! I – we have been out of our minds with worry. Your father has even gone over to England to look for you!"
"I don't understand. Why? What was the big deal? Susan knew what I was doing. Why didn't you ring her?"

"That one! She was like the three wise monkeys! According to her, she knew nothing – it was like you were the bloody Marie Celeste! There one minute, gone the next."

"Oh, forget her! She is just a moody cow. If anybody should be upset it should be me ... not her! She made the decision, did not consult me, did not bother about how I might feel or even consider that I might be interested!"

With that he took off the ruck sack, and seemed to his mother that he was close to tears. She quickly picked up the bag, linked arms and steered him out through the main hotel doors and off towards the family's own spacious living quarters adjacent to the main body of the hotel. The hotel was a purpose built attractive structure, which stood in quite extensive grounds, with its sweeping drive. This led through a pair of ornate wrought iron gates onto a quiet country backroad, though this, in reality, was 50 yards from the main arterial road leading to Cork City proper. The hotel, then, was close enough to civilisation, but remote enough to be attractive to people who wanted to pretend they were far away from the madding crowd but who got withdrawal symptoms or the heebie-jeebies if they were not within striking distance of shops, cars and crowds.

Maeve and Kevin's own home was the original farmhouse which had been extensively modernised, but still held the exterior charm and rustic qualities of by-gone years. Inside it was tastefully decorated and furnished, but still homely and happily somewhat dishevelled and 'lived in'. As they reached the front door, Mon suddenly pulled his arm free, and raced back towards the hotel, returning almost immediately with his bicycle, which had been the trusty steed that had conveyed him all the way. He had cycled from the East Midlands, right across England, and on through Wales, and then onwards across virtually the whole breadth of the Southern half of Ireland to the South West of the country. His only rest had been on the rough and windy sea crossing, during which Mon had remained on deck to avoid the smell of the engines, the smell of the beer and the smell of the vomit which could cause nausea in the hardiest of sailors. It had not been that many years since cattle and livestock shared the journey, with the beasts down in the hold and the passengers on the floors above.

Once they were safely inside, Maeve immediately picked up a phone and attempted to put through a call to Eddie, but got no answer. She would have to try later …. *(Obviously I was by that stage well on my way up to Nottingham, so she unfortunately was out of luck. It was a pity for myself as well, since I would at least then have known that one of my imagined 'victims' was alive and kicking.)*

Far from realising that he had started a proper hue and cry, he seemed quite oblivious to his mother's sleepless nights! He pulled off his boots, discarded his jacket and ripping his shirt off as he went, he said "God I need a shower! I am stinking! …… What's for dinner – I could eat a manky cat!" With that, he was gone, bits of his clothing providing a trail – like crumbs for Hansel and Gretel – until he disappeared into the bathroom, and his voice could be heard singing loudly and whooping as the refreshing hot water rained down on him.

Maeve was of course delighted that the wanderer had returned, but was now anxious to get hold of Kevin. She could not ring him. The only contact point she had was Eddie's and he was not there - and neither was Eddie! She would have to wait until he rang her – which he might not do until he had found Mon – which he would not do now, because Mon was here – singing his fecking head off in the bathroom …. Thank God! She remembered to offer a word of thanks to all of the saints she had entreated to find him, and remembered to ask them now, perhaps, to turn their attention to getting a message to her poor husband to call her – and come home quickly!

Chapter 23: Meanwhile in England the search continues!

I had reached my destination – hoping that was not a true description for 'the end of the road'. I had absolutely no idea what I would do if neither Susan nor Kevin were there. I was completely unfamiliar with the area, and it would have been a long way to drive for nothing.

The house itself had no lights on – but it was only two o'clock in the afternoon (I am not a fast driver!) so that told me nothing in itself, but the fact that there were full milk bottles still sitting on the doorstep was not a reassuring sight. Anyway, there was nothing else to do but at least knock on the door. I had already told myself that it was a waste of time; I had had a wasted journey; I was foolish to not think the matter through more sensibly before I set out …. all completely futile thoughts, given that I was there and no magic wand was going to alter that fact.

On my third knock, a head came out of an upstairs window. "Yes – Can I help you?"
"Oh, yes. Thanks. I was looking for Susan, or Eamon – are they in?"

"Oh, blimey. You are the second one! I haven't a clue! They live in the flat on the bottom – I'm up here – nearer to the stars! I haven't seen Mon for weeks now – two, three maybe.   Sue was here – I saw her Tuesday for certain, because I was late for a lecture and we caught the same bus.   …….. Come to think of it, she had a kind of hold-all with her – could be she was going away for a few days. I got off at the stop in the high street, she stayed on. I said 'Tata' and that was the last. I told all that to the other bloke – he came yesterday…. Mind you he was on foot – looked most put out. Long way out of town, I guess, for nothing.   Couldn't help him really. Don't know what else I can tell you."

Beginning to fear the worst for Mon, and believing that Susan was, by now, well and truly gone far away – as far as possible, one supposed, I was stumped.   Had Kevin returned to London?   I needed to find a phone box and call home to see if he was there.

There would have been no point hanging around, I thought, for him when he came up empty at the house. Surely he would just go back to my place?

got back in the car. I sat for a few minutes, obviously now at a loss as to what to do next. I hate to say it, but my decision was to do what all English people do when perplexed, disappointed, shocked, or otherwise discombobulated …. I decided to find somewhere to get a cup of tea! It would give me time to think, and I had rushed out in any case without breakfast. I had no idea that fear, frustration, confusion made me hungry, but suddenly I convinced myself that a good hearty lunch would help me think what to do next. It was, at least, a way of killing time before I had to head back southwards again – a morning wasted, petrol wasted, nothing gained, nothing resolved.

I found a café not very far away from the house, in a pretty and surprisingly bustling high street. I picked a table quite close to the window, and after a very short time a woman called over from behind the serving counter "We're self-service now, ducks!" In my embarrassment, I immediately apologised for my stupidity (though how I supposed to know, and why I should be apologising, I have no idea – the English disease, again, I suppose!). I went across to the counter, and reading the menu which was written up in chalk on the wall, I said I would have the Cottage pie. "Will that be with peas, or with carrots?" To be honest, I could not have cared less at that moment because my desire for food had completely deserted me and

I wished I had just turned the car and headed for home. But here I was, and the thick set, henna dyed, woman with her drawn on alarming eyebrows, prominent rouged cheeks and bright scarlet lips, was obviously awaiting an answer! Despite the fact that there were only two other people in the place, both sitting as far apart as it was possible to be, both sitting nursing just a cup and saucer, with absolutely no sign whatsoever of an actual meal, I was obviously intruding on her very busy life.

"Peas, I suppose" I said. "Mushy or marrowfat?" she said. Who cares I thought, but obviously, being an elderly, well-mannered and well-brought up English woman, I merely said "Oh yes, thank you. Well …. no on second thoughts, I'll have the carrots." It seemed less traumatic – the thought of deciding between mushy and marrowfat, was suddenly more than I could stand. She merely shrugged, and yelled through to the kitchen, presumably the other side of the menu wall, "Cottage, and carrots …. One". She then returned to her previous occupation of reading 'Woman's Own 'and I returned to my window table, not knowing whether to laugh or cry, and feeling like doing both simultaneously – that, I think, is known as hysteria!

I moved my food around my plate a bit so as not to give the impression that the food was nasty or that I was dissatisfied in some way, but if I had been hungry before, the tide had subsided and I found that I could no longer stomach anything, let alone an enormous plate of mashed potato, hiding a reasonably miserly amount of grisly minced meat – not sure of the animal – containing copious amounts of onions and runny gravy. The 'carrots' were very obviously tinned, and precious little effort had been made to drain them before they were plonked on the plate because the whole meal could have done the breaststroke and swum around the plate a few times. I can truthfully say that, even if I had continued to be ravenous, I still would have found it difficult to persuade myself to tuck into the joys before me! It was good then that I was no longer hungry.

I waited what seemed like an appropriate amount of time, and then went up to the counter and said "Can I pay you please". Red lips said "Everything all right?" I said "Yes, very nice, thank you. I have small appetite, but it was delicious". She looked at me as though she thought I might be being sarcastic, and then seemed to lose interest, merely shrugging, taking the proffered money, and returning to her magazine. I left, wishing I had never gone in!

Back out on to the high street, I recognised the familiar sign for the post office, and decided that sufficient time had elapsed and that surely Kevin would have returned by then. I went in and found the telephone boxes over in the corner, and convincing myself that he would be there and would answer immediately, I dialled my own telephone number. It rang and it rang and it rang. Even when I KNEW that there was obviously nobody there, I still kept hanging on, not wishing to accept the situation, because that meant that I was even more in a quandary than I had been. Was he still up here? Had he already returned to my house, and then gone and got the boat-train back to Ireland? Had he found Mon? Had the found Susan? Just what was the situation now. I contemplated telephoning Maeve, but what would I tell her? I had absolutely no idea where her son was and now I had absolutely no idea where her husband was either!

I left the post office worse off than when I went in, and now completely at a loss as to what to do next.

I am not a church goer – not anti-religion, just not convinced and never having felt the need to find any form of strength that I did not have within myself. I have no idea why I went into the big, ornate and elaborate building – to me a building of architectural interest, but with no other kind of draw or significance. Inside the vast, incense smelling – cavernous – church, I could see dotted about the shrines and dedications, lit with clusters of lit candles and novena lights. It seemed peaceful and tranquil and I was in need of a quiet place to think, to come to terms with my current predicament – and to try to be less concerned with my own predicament than to appreciate the implications for others: for Mon, for Maeve, for Kevin. Here was I feeling sorry for myself because of a wasted journey – a few hours out of an otherwise uncommitted and empty schedule – and others were potentially facing the worse moments of their lives – if for Mon it was not already too late!

I sat at the back of the church, my eyes damp, an embroidered handkerchief clutched in a ball in my hand, and I tried to empty my mind, to get to some plain where I could think clearly, get back to my normal practical, down-to-earth and methodical self. I was fed up with this tearful, wishy-washy, sentimentalist that I had become!
I heard a movement way over to the side of the church, to where a side chapel was illuminated, the intricate stained glass window showing a saint – I am not good at identifying saints – it never having come within my 'need to know' parameters – but this one, I did somehow recognise. He had his foot on the head of a snake, and other serpents were crawling away as though in fear. It was obviously Saint Patrick who chased all the snakes out of Ireland. I

had seen the picture many times when I stayed with Maeve, because she had almost the self-same picture hanging in the lobby of the hotel – not quite so large, or course, but the same in miniature.

As I looked across, a figure stood up from where it had been kneeling, and went across to light a candle, dropping the coins into the metal box before taking the taper and lighting the flame. The figure genuflected, and then turned, head bowed, walking slowly, shoulders stooped, in obvious distress, down the side aisle of the church. The figure was almost at the door when I suddenly realised who it was. As I said, I am not a 'believer' as such, but I almost said a prayer that day – it was Kevin! I called across, my voice sounding alien in the total silence of the vast church, and it startled him. He looked around, almost as though one of the pictures, or the statues, had called his name, and I got up as quickly as I could and went over to him, out of the darkness. He was, naturally, taken aback, certainly not expecting me to be in Southwich, let alone standing here, well over a 100 miles from where I should be. I would like to think that I was in the right place at the right time. I was there just when he needed somebody to be there the most. I know it did not have to be me, but since I had a means of transport, and I was, at least temporarily, his housekeeper it was handy. Even more, I think, it was welcome that he did not have to explain anything, so I was perhaps as good as anyone, and better than most. He actually hugged me, before breaking down, and collapsing at my feet. Looking at his gaunt and ashen face, I knew that he was not well – not just heart-sick, but physically unwell. I managed to get him into a pew, as best I could, and went back outside, found a telephone box, and called for an ambulance. Though my specialty has been psychiatry over the years, that does not prevent me from remembering my more general medical training, and I just knew that there was something very, very wrong with Kevin Clarkin.

The ambulance arrived some fifteen minutes later, by which time, Kevin had found his strength again, and protested vehemently when loaded on the stretcher and moved into the vehicle. I said I would follow on, since I needed to collect my car, but would be there within minutes. His last words to me before they drove away were

"Eddie, Dr. Tennyson, don't for God's sake tell Maeve!"

Such a responsibility! I should tell her! I needed to tell her! But here was Kevin vehemently instructing me not to do so. I have never taken orders in my life – and I was not going to start now. I would consider my options when I had caught up with him at the hospital, but my immediate reaction was "Kevin, I hear what you say, but …."

I collected my car, which was parked outside the post office, and eventually found the hospital. It took longer than I thought possible, since the hospital was really not that large – but then I am a Londoner and am used to the numerous and vast sprawling medical facilities of the capital - to track Kevin down. He was looking much better by now, and was anxious to persuade the doctors that he was fit to go. They were determined to do a number of tests before they discharged him, but he seemed unnecessarily agitated by this, and was inclined to just up sticks and leave. The presence of mind of a nurse to remove his shoes when he was brought in made his 'flight' impracticable. I guess she did this for more ordinary reasons than any premonition that they might provide a diversionary tactic to detain him, but having   accidentally left them in the Emergency Department, it served a useful purpose anyway.

They decided to sedate him, and carried out such tests as were considered necessary. I waited – still trying to decide whether to call his wife or not. Eventually one of the doctors came out to speak with me, assuming I was a relative, and I did not disillusion him. He started to speak about 'his condition' and how the fact that he had been overdoing things had made his situation more unstable. He asked about his medication – at which point, I had to come clean and explain – not the whole story, obviously, but I said that he had stayed with me for a couple of days because he was over in the UK visiting his son and daughter-in-law, but that, unfortunately, they were away at the moment. They had decided to keep him in hospital, and asked if there was any way that I could bring some nightwear, shaving things, etc. for him. Not as easy as all that, I thought, given that they were all at least 100 miles away – even if they existed in the UK. For all I knew they might all be much further away than that – in County Cork, Ireland – where his poor wife, remained still clueless about his current situation, and still clueless about the whereabouts of her son. I definitely needed to ring her. There was no getting away from it now. Things had taken on a whole different complexion!

I went out of the waiting area, and enquired from one of the porters where the nearest telephone box was. I was told that there was a telephone just outside the main entrance. No more excuses, it had to be done! I rang Maeve.

Chapter 24: If it smells it is not necessarily off!

I could do no more now. I booked into an hotel, knowing that though Kevin had said 'go home' and Maeve had said the same, because she would be over the next day – and she would fly, so would get there quickly – I still did not feel at liberty to just abandon him. I would go when Maeve got there.

Naturally I was more than relieved – delighted in fact – to hear that Mon had turned up and was alive and kicking, and not a hair harmed on his head. It made me question the whole pantomime and wonder if all of it had not been some kind of mental aberration that I had got sucked into. Gladys had taken me in, and I had fallen for it, hook, line and sinker. I would be a laughing stock. But I was relieved too, of course I was. Selfishly I was aware that because so much of my retired life had been taken up with the 'gene' mystery, my days might now need filling with something else. Although I had not spelled it out, because, obviously there were other people to consider, my intention had been to write 'the definitive book' either exposing the myth, or unveiling the concept, of 'the pernicious gene', the 'murder gene'. I was not sure now that that was appropriate, since I was not sure that either premise was sound – I had to consider that Gladys/Maggie et al had not set out to 'fool' anybody – no expose was required, but neither did the 'gene' exist, but had been conjured up because of coincidence, histrionics and gullibility – not least my own!

I had time on my hands in Southwick, and out of sheer boredom and perhaps a little bit of wanting to hold on to a good story, I returned to check whether Susan had returned.

The milk was gone off the doorstep, perhaps a good sign, but then it might have been Mr. Upstairs' milk for all I knew. Nevertheless, I rang the bell, and low and behold, the door was opened almost immediately by Susan herself.

She seemed, for her, quite animated, and came to the door cheerily enough. She was surprised, obviously, to see me not only because we had had no contact for quite some time, but also here we were in quite a different part of the country to where we expected to find each other. She was hospitable enough, however, and invited me in quite readily.

Her travel bag – obviously the one that her neighbour had mentioned – was still on the floor inside the living room door, so I thought she had perhaps not been back all that long – wherever she had been off to.

"Well, this is a surprise!" she said. "Can I get you a cup of something – I don't have tea, I'm afraid, Mon and I decided to ban all drinks with stimulants in – coffee the same. I've got fruit juice … or filtered water?

Out of politeness, I said that water would be welcome. Still at the back of my mind, despite myself, and despite even poo-pooing my own stupidity, I was nevertheless somewhat suspicious of any kind of food or drink that Susan might offer me. It almost built up to a kind of Russian roulette game in my head! I dared to drink! A test of the theory! A proof of the 'gene' theory. If I died, then the proof would have been achieved! Needless to say, nothing happened.

"Funny you should come today. I've just come back from visiting Helen. Did they tell you, that they are letting her out! Isn't it great! …. Was it you here yesterday too? Ray, upstairs, said somebody came round – in fact he said two people came round …. separate times, one Wednesday, the other yesterday.

"Yes, that was me. The other one was Kevin. He came looking for Mon."

"Mon? He's in Ireland, isn't he? We had a bit of a barney …. Stupid really! We've spoken on the phone since, and I think he is all right. Bloody annoying he is sometimes, though! He thinks it's me, but he has to remember that we ain't married and he cannot boss me about."

"I think he cycled to Ireland – so it took a long time."

"Cycled! To Ireland! Bloody hell, he must be mad! I can understand why he didn't fly, 'cos he wanted to take the bike, but he could have gone on the bleedin' train and boat. Cycle! What a dope! Fit, though, eh! He's a soppy sod, isn't he! I love the silly bugger …. Cycled …. All the way to soddin' Ireland, what a laugh."

I have to admit that Susan sounded disarmingly full of love and admiration for the 'silly sod' and her face lit up when she spoke about him. It was almost endearing, and I began to really warm to her. But then my head took me back to her news about Helen.

"When did you hear that they were going to release Helen?"

"I guess, now that Nan's gone, I must be her 'next of kin' – strange as that sounds. I know that place where she is thinks we are all barmy! Not just Helen. They think the whole thing's a pantomime. My mum kills her mum, she kills my mum, and here we are all good pals together. ……. They can't get their head around it. I think – though you might know better than me, being a shrink and all that, with your foot in their door – that they kept her in longer because they thought the whole family was nuts, but they couldn't quite give it a name. I suppose from an outsider's perspective, it does seem strange. I cannot give them any answers – it's just how it has always been. I've spoken to Mon about it lots of times - him being practically brought up with Hel – but it's not really logical, so we don't come to any conclusions. Just have to accept it for what it is. Strange, just not normal, perhaps. But fact, just the same. ….. Anyway, so Helen is free as from next Thursday – the 20$_{th}$, I think that is. She is planning to go stay with Maeve and Kevin – Maeve offered years ago – not sure if she thought the offer would ever be taken up or not, but if it was an empty gesture, she will get a rude awakening! So I've said, since Mon is there anyway, that I will go with her. I can stay for a few days, settle her in, and then me and Mon can come home."

For some reason, some selfish reason, I was miffed that all these plans had been made without me! I grasped at the one 'fact' that I had not been told but that I really had no right to have been kept informed of …. Simply, in a childish way, to get my own back.

"When did Gladys die?"

"Die? Bloody hell, no, she ain't dead! She's gone to stay with Connie's daughter in New Zealand for a couple of months. She lost her baby, you know – Jessie did – the second one she lost. This one died at three weeks, the other one was two years old. Gladys said she had to go over there – she seemed to get very agitated about it. I was not sure what she thought she could do about it, but she was determined to go. No bloody idea how she afforded the fare, but I think – not that it compensates because she was in a right state about it – but I think she got insurance when Grandad George died. They hadn't been together for years, but she still had kept the insurance up on him. Lucky, eh. The timing was perfect."

"I never met George. What did he die of?"

"Not sure – heart I think.   He had been ill for ages, but got worse quite suddenly, and just pegged it!   What with that and Auntie Connie and the other George – but I think that George was spelled different, Jorge of something – anyway he died too – last year, caravan burnt out, they got him out, but not in time.   Connie was heartbroken.   They've had a bit of a hard time, bless 'em. Anyway, both Connie and Nan are in New Zealand.   Back September time, I think. I hope so, anyway, because Mon and me have decided to get married – I spoke to him on the phone yesterday, and we've decided that it is about time."

I was brought down to earth with a bump at this news, which suddenly reminded me – not a moment too soon – about Kevin.

"Kevin is in Southwick hospital – he got taken ill yesterday.   Went there by ambulance."

"Oh Gawd.   What happened.   Is he going to be all right!   What a time for Mon to be so far away.   What's wrong with him?   Are they keeping him in …… I had better go up there.   I'll get my coat.   Will you drive me?   Sorry to ask, but ….. might as well take advantage of your being here, eh?"

I was almost glad to be doing something and stood up immediately. I needed thinking time. I needed to get out of the house. I was not sure what I needed, but it was probably breathing space from anybody remotely linked to the Barber family!

I drove Susan up to the hospital and left her with her prospective father-in-law, and went out to get some fresh air. I wish I smoked, or drank to excess. My brain just would not stop whirling. I found myself back at the church – no real sanctuary for an agnostic, but it was quiet, and dark and virtually empty. Perhaps Elizabeth might tell me what to do! Nobody living was going to be of any help. It was either divine intervention, a whisper from the spirit world, or spirits of a more liquid description!

Chapter 25: A problem shared is a problem halved – NOT!

Maeve arrived on a very late flight that night, and managed to identify a train for the onwards journey. Since Susan was at the hospital, we had arranged that I would be at her house waiting for a phone call from Maeve and I would pick her up from the station and take her to the hospital. I had plenty time to kill and spent this carrying out an almost forensic examination of the house – looking for anything that might conceivably give me some idea of whether Mon was in dire peril. Needless to say I found everything and I found nothing! What for heaven's sake constituted a danger? I couldn't remove the cutlery, the matches, the pillows – there were any number of ways to kill, any number of things, completely innocent things, scattered about the house that under certain circumstances were 'weapons'.

Eventually the phone rang, and I set off to the mainline station – about 20 miles away – to pick up Maeve. She had had to wait for me, but was full of gratitude for my assistance, and remarkably stoical under the circumstances. I was reluctant to broach any 'delicate' subject during our journey – and was not even sure whether she knew about Kevin's illness. According to the doctor, it was certainly beyond the stage when it would have been picked up and diagnosed by a doctor – but only if Kevin had consulted a doctor. I had insufficient knowledge of the man, or the medical facilities in County Cork, to know whether he was likely to have 'consulted a doctor' or not. I decided not to discuss the matter and kept to the bare facts – that I had, luckily, gone into the church, and that he had collapsed, and I had rung an ambulance. I did say that I thought it was a kind of miracle that we were both there at the same time – I did not even elaborate on how very very lucky that really was, since I am agnostic, certainly not religious and definitely not Catholic! I am always impressed – envious perhaps – of people with a real faith. How comforting and reassuring that must be. Maeve said, quite matter-of-factly "A miracle yes, perhaps, but I had said lots of prayers to St. Patrick and the other saints to look after them, so I am not surprised."

I said that I had subsequently gone to see whether Susan had returned and had taken her up to sit with Kevin. Anything else – any other important matter – would have to wait for a more appropriate time and more suitable circumstances.

When we arrived at the hospital, Susan was relieved to be able to hand over the vigil – which was now more of a 'keeping company' exercise than anything else – to Maeve. Kevin was equally delighted to see her, but pretended that he was annoyed that she had been brought all this way, for nothing, because 'he was grand!' 'no bother! 'perfectly fine altogether'. 'lot of fuss over nothing!'. But he clung to her hand and nothing could disguise the relief that he got from her presence. She also was able to tell him – which Susan had already done – that Mon was fine and that the silly eejit cycled all the way home – it took him nearly two weeks! Apparently he did stop off with a couple of friends en route who had had met during his travels at various times. He quite enjoyed the pedal, apparently, she said, but was not tempted to repeat it in the near future, and was expecting to be returning to the UK in a more conventional – and less exhausting – fashion.

Susan had told Kevin that she and Mon were going to get married, which was a surprise to Maeve, who was astonished that Mon had said nothing to her about it during his time at home. In fact, he had implied, when he arrived, that he had embarked on the cycle ride to escape from Susan because of something she had done, or not done, or was going to do ….. Young love! How well she remembered it! Down in the cafeteria, I sat with Susan and for once she seemed adult and serious and seemed to have something on her mind.

I bought us both tea – which she accepted despite its harmful properties – and big fat fattening cakes, which she also seemed ready to devour.

"Eddie" she said, "About this family curse thing.... Do you think it is real? It really scares me. I want to laugh at it, but then things happen and I get worried. Do you think it's real?"

I was glad to be able to talk about it but perhaps not to her. Given my previous – and possibly even present – mistrust of Susan herself, it seemed both dangerous and hypocritical. Did I tell her that I thought it was rubbish, and encourage her to feel safe and unsuspected; did I say I thought there was every chance that there was a 'murder gene' and make fact out of fiction? She then put me at an even greater disadvantage, because as I looked at this hardnosed, in-your-face and together young woman I saw big tears welling up and beginning to flow down her face. She was surreptitiously trying to wipe these away, turning her head to avoid me seeing, which made them all the more powerful. Not an act. Not a ploy. Those were real tears; tears cried by somebody who was in real distress, tears of somebody who had every right to be concerned because until she had secured the right answer from me, the so called expert, she could not move on with her life.

I instinctively put a hand out and brushed away the tears with the back of my hand, and said as gently as I could, that I just did not know, though every bone in my body, and brain in my head was saying that the whole concept was nuts – bananas, absolutely daft!

I said that I had more or less made up my mind that all of the 'deaths', apart of course from Elizabeth and her mother, had been just coincidences, and that birth was a precarious time; infants did die – sad as it was – but other families had probably lost just as many children but were not putting it down to some kind of genetic mutation. I said that I had been thrown – as she may have noticed – by the sudden/accidental deaths of the two Georges, and the fortuitous acquisition of the insurance monies – those were still 'worrying' me a bit. I did think, though, on reflection, that it was possible that Gladys (and Connie – and maybe they conspired together?) had seen the whole 'gene' myth as a good excuse for them to get some cash….. you know the kind of thing "I could not help myself, it's my nature!"

I was pleased to see Susan laugh at that one. She knew as well as I did that the family was strong enough, clever enough, single-minded enough to have carried out those two 'murders'. They would have had nothing to do with a 'gene'. They would have had everything to do with opportunity, motivation and 'balls'. For all I knew, Gladys could have made up the entire myth about the 'gene' and thought it was a good laugh to send me off on a wild goose chase – a wild gene chase! Susan laughed once more.

I was obviously still not sure about Susan, but I was 'warming' to her, warts and all, just like Helen. She told me that she had been visiting Helen for the past year – and the two girls had apparently had a good game with the staff, being mysterious and 'strange'. Susan would ask whoever was on duty specific questions, such as when is the final 'ward' round of the night, what time is the first in the morning. Can Helen please have some extra sharp pencils and a Stanley knife. Questions with no other motivation other than to 'wind up' the staff and make them think there was some kind of 'plan' afoot. Susan was looking forward to having Helen out again, and significantly too Helen – or so she said – was now able to accept that she would be free, and was not only resigned to this, but was positively anticipating it with some degree of glee. I suddenly realised that I had written to Helen every few weeks, but had not actually visited her for the past seven or eight months. That having been said, if Susan had been visiting for the past year, Helen had certainly kept that quiet. I wonder why? Now it was my time to see worries when there were none. Why should she tell me? Perhaps she thought I would not approve. She could have been right. But what right did I have to approve or disapprove?

All the time I had been thinking, Susan had been talking and I must have looked as though I was listening intently. Suddenly she said "What do you think? Am I wrong? If it is all a silly story, then I am pissing off Mon for absolutely no reason, and I do love him – I really do!"

I was embarrassed then and tried desperately to hedge, trying to look as if I was thinking, as if I was weighing a matter of real significance in my head. I may well have been, but I had absolutely no idea what she was asking me.

I was saved when Maeve appeared and said "Susan, any chance of me getting a bit of a wash and brush up at your place – Kevin is sleeping."

"Absolutely ….. of course. Here you are, here's my key. Make yourself at home." She searched in her bag for her front door key and was beginning to panic, when I realised that it was I that had the key since I had been there last waiting for Maeve to arrive at the station. I went to offer this to Susan, but she said

"Eddie, you take her. We would just have to get the bus, and they are not that frequent from here. Keep the key – you have the car. I will stay here in case Kevin wakes up. I have a book. I am fine, really I am."

I looked at her, and said "that makes sense, if you don't mind. Have you got enough money for more tea and a sandwich or something? I have change if you need it -- here take this ..." I handed over a pound note and she tried to object, but I insisted. I was very relieved that 'the question' had been forgotten. Hopefully the next time she asked it – if there was a next time – I would have listened properly. Maeve and I set off for Susan's house, leaving Susan to have a sandwich for a little while, and then go up and sit with Kevin. As luck would have it, he had been put into a side room when he arrived because of their worry over his condition. Most of the other parts of the hospital had quite strict and somewhat miserly visiting times, but nobody seemed to be too fussed about the smaller, private, rooms. They were pleased, I think, that they did not need to keep popping in to ensure that he was alive and kicking.

When we arrived back at the house, Maeve went off to have a wash and to change her clothes. She had not brought much, but she felt a bit 'travel-worn' and was glad to get into something else. She looked brighter when she came back and we sat for a while. I made a drink – squash, obviously! We had a laugh over the ban on tea and coffee since she knew that at home, at that very moment, Mon was likely swilling down his umpteenth cup of the day, and I knew for a fact that Susan had finished off the tea in the hospital canteen without demur either. We decided that they would probably declare themselves vegetarian next, which might last for a month or two!

After a lull in the conversation, I noticed that Maeve was actually crying. I reached across and took her hand. I knew what was wrong, but preferred her to tell me, rather than rush in like a bull at a gate.

"He's dying, Eddie" she said. Cancer .... I've – we've known for about four months. He tries to pretend – not that it not happening, he's anything but an ostrich – but that he can still manage, still go on as normal, until the ... end. He hasn't even told Connor or Siobhan – and has forbidden me to say anything. They still expect him to work as he did before – and he does – but it takes a lot out of him. I was worried sick about him coming over here. I was going to come instead, but Connor said why did Kevin not go, I was more useful back home because of Siobhan being sick – and because of the new baby. Kevin still forbade me from saying anything. Now we will both be in trouble because Connor will feel bad because he sent him off even though he is so sick. Oh Eddie! How will I go on without him!" She wept properly, and I let her. It was best for her to cry. It was clear that she rarely was allowed to do so, since she wouldn't in front of Kevin, and the rest of the family did not even know.

After a while, she blew her nose, said "what an old fool I am – we'd better go" and gathered up her coat and bag, leaving, I noticed, a £20 note under an ornament for Susan, and headed for the door.

We returned to the hospital in time to see a commotion around Kevin's room. He had taken a turn for the worst and they had asked Susan to go while they sorted things out. She seemed bemused and almost in a kind of stupor, just standing outside in the corridor, almost in the way of the rushing medics, but not having the sense to realise it.

I grabbed her and said "What happened?"

She said "I don't know! Suddenly an alarm on one of the machines started to go off, and people just rushed in, and threw me out. He had been awake. He had been talking – just kind of mumbling, but it sort of made sense – you know "What's going on? I need to get up! Where's Mon? "

She started to cry then, pulled me to one side, so that a distraught Maeve (who was being taken off to a family room by one of the staff) could not hear and said "Oh Eddie, he said "What have you done to Mon?" I was in shock! What did he mean? Does he know about the family? Does he think I might have … I might have … No, no… " With that her words were completely engulfed in sobs and gulps and I was left not knowing whether to stay and comfort her or go and comfort Maeve. It was also quite dangerous to take Susan off to the same place that Maeve was. If Susan tried to quiz Maeve, then nothing could be gained when Maeve was obviously beyond upset anyway.

If nothing else, Susan had the family trait of failing to really empathise with others – she only saw her own grief, her own troubles, she had no realisation that now was not the time to raise such questions – even though they might be of paramount importance to her.

I had started to warm to Susan, started to believe her perhaps, but the fact that she was with Kevin when he was suddenly taken bad was a sobering reminder that I just did not know …. I just did not KNOW!

If he had given her some indication – which she definitely said he had – that he thought she might have 'done something' to Mon, and thus let her know that he knew the family secret, then would she act on that? If there was a family secret she might. IF!

BUT he was a cancer patient. He was seriously ill. He was dying. He had been seriously overdoing it, gadding about the country, his mind in turmoil; he had probably not eaten; he may well have not slept. Let's be logical! He had also been 'taken bad' when he was with me, and I know that I am not part of the 'family secret'! Why then am I blaming Susan? Just because of what may be a completely fictitious and fabricated bit of mischief on the part of her grandmother.

Once again I pondered on the what question had she asked me earlier? Would it have helped or hindered my dilemma?

It was a close run thing, but on that occasion Kevin recovered, and after five days in hospital, he was allowed to fly back, with Maeve, to spend what time he had in the comfort of his own home. He lived another three months, and died peacefully, surrounded by all his children – some of whom had returned from far flung parts of the world. There too was Helen, now released from her incarceration and pleased to be able to be there to say goodbye to Kevin who she had always had a soft spot for, and who had always treated her as one of his own.

Mon had been there too, but then he and Susan had returned home to Southwick so that Susan could start the new term at the local college where she was intending to study midwifery.

Some weeks before this, Susan had telephoned me to ask if she could come and visit because she wanted to talk to me. I said of course.

I cooked her dinner and we had a pleasant evening together, with me trying to not mention the PG!

However, after dinner, when we were sitting quietly, she asked me whether I had had a chance to think about her question to me in the hospital in Southwick. Having thought that I had escaped unscathed, I was horrified that here was I being forced to admit my complete lack of attention, and the fact that I had no idea what the 'question' had been.

Thinking on my feet, I said "In the light of events since, just recap for me the situation, and whether any of that has changed any aspect of the situation."

It was pure waffle, but it seemed to work. If she twigged my motives, she was too polite to say, but I hope she did not.

"OK. Well, as I said, I love Mon, and most of the time Mon loves me – and that is quite difficult sometimes – I have to admit!

I have lived now – since I was about 8 when great grandma Maggie died – knowing about this silly 'gene' thing. Maggie's bed had been moved downstairs to the front room when she was ill so that she could look out of the window and see people going by. When she was really ill – not long before she died - I don't really know when that was because they sent me off to stay with Auntie Lena in Canvey – I had made a den under the washing between the sideboard and the armchair, and they did not know that I was there.

Anyway, I did not really understand much – at the time – but I remembered the words, so when I was older, obviously, I was able to join the dots. I don't think I really believed any of it – and if I did I thought it was a bit of a laugh! It had never really entered my own head then that it affected me. I knew that I was not particularly girly, bit of a tomboy, but I never had any kind of urge to hurt or kill anybody – I was not even all that handy with me mitts! At school I would argue a lot, and I was gobby, but I was not one for fighting or hurting people. But that kind of thing plays on your mind.

Then you were around, the person with the 'expertise' and you seemed to believe Gran when she told you – you actually took her seriously, well at least you started to look into it – to research it. I know she was impressed by that. She thought she had your ear all right! She felt important! I think that until you took it seriously, she was more inclined to take it all with a pinch of salt and I know for a fact that she had embroidered the story over time – it seemed, like Pinocchio's nose, to grow and grow, to get more and more elaborate, the more often she told it. Nan KNEW Greatnan could be a bit melodramatic – and she was always one for seeing wrongs when there weren't any – so I think that Auntie Glad over time had become more likely to not believe her than to believe her, but she was enjoying the story and the thrill of it all …. Until you seemed to consider it all really possible!

You found all that out about the French girls, and all that. You thought she might have killed those babies, didn't you? With your stories and Great Nan's stories, I know me Nan convinced herself that there was more than a good story in it, that Aggie-Maggie might have been telling the truth.

I've spoken to Helen a lot in recent years, and we both feel the same. We think that it is all rubbish. I am sorry Eddie – Dr. Tennyson – I know that sounds disrespectful but it has to be said. It has been ruining too many people's lives - including yours even – for too long!

When it finally came to me being afraid to have children of my own, and chasing away Mon because of my stupid worries, I had to talk to you. That's why I spoke to you when we were alone in the hospital canteen. Mon and me had had a row. He wanted to get married and I said no, because we were all right as we were. He said he did not want to have kids without us being married, and I said I couldn't/wouldn't have kids any way. He said why, I said because. He said because was no answer and I ended up telling him that I was cursed and if I had children I might kill them, because I had some deadly gene that turned us all into murderers.   He laughed.   He just laughed.   I got mad, but he couldn't stop laughing.   I threw a knife at him, which he ducked. That proved to me that I was a potential killer, he said it just proved that I had a foul temper and I was a lousy shot.   Finally, I said I did not want to see him, or talk to him anymore, and he should find another place to live.   He said, thanks, but it was his place to begin with, so if I didn't love him anymore, that I should move out, though he would rather that I stayed because he loved me even if I had a silly gene!

"He had been talking about going to see his Mum and Dad for a while, and I had promised to go with him but kept finding excuses. I don't know why.   I think they are nice people –   I just can't feel comfortable with myself, the thought of the future, of kids, just scares me.   I worry that I could really hurt somebody – Mon, or children …. Eddie, it's really scary!

"Then, one day, out of the blue, when I had been really REALLY horrible to him, he said "Right, I will have to marry you, gene or no gene, because you are the only one who makes me laugh.   I am going home to Ireland to tell me Ma and Pa to get ready for a wedding and in the meantime you can sort out your head once and for all and tell silly Jean to pack her bags and vacate the premises.

"That was why I spoke to you.

"So … here goes!   I shall ask you again.   My important question to you, then, is: Can you **prove** any of this Gene business?

"It seems to me that it is not the gene that is blighting my bloomin' life but the uncertainty of it all.   I could, to some extent, ignore what Great Nan – Aggie Maggie –   said, she was a bit crackers at the end anyway, and me Nan can be a bit – no, a lot – of a drama queen -   I think she quite enjoyed the 'specialness' of the whole thing, but you – you are a doctor, an educated person, somebody who should know whether the whole thing is complete rubbish!

"If you are convinced – even half convinced -   how can I dare risk it! How can I bring children into the world – how can I be near anybody – forever.   What if I get fed up?   What if they annoy me – or I just get bored.   What do I do then?   Do I just decide to kill them?   It's the bloody 'what if's' that really get to me.

"I started going to see Helen – because …. Well because, surely she understands.   She could, maybe, give me some idea whether she thought she had done what she done because she was, kind of, programmed – hot-wired – to do it, or whether ….   I don't know, whether she thought it was just something she had to do because of what had happened to her mum. Did she, I just wondered, think that she would have just picked on somebody else – without the reason – if you get my drift.

"I know I am not explaining this very clearly, but somehow Helen understood. She is quite clear, I think. She says…. Don't get me wrong – and don't think badly of her, Eddie …, but she is grateful to you, and knows that you have been really kind to her over the years, but she thinks …. Well, she thinks, that you have been taken for a ride …. by Nan, she thinks. She was not even sure that it had started off with great gran (though I could say that was true, 'cos I actually heard part of the conversation, so Nan was truthful to that extent. Helen still thinks, though, that if that's the case, it was Aggie Maggie who made it up – Gawd knows why! Seems a really silly and pointless game, at that time, when you are just about to kick the bucket. But then she was a funny – and looking back – a bit of a nasty old biddy! Do you know she used to pull your hair - really pull it - pretending to comb it. She had this thing about hair! Nasty she could be – despite her bloody sweets and smiles! Anyway, Helen says that since she – Helen - has never had any other desire to kill anybody else, neither before, nor after, it was Great Nan being sensationalist. Just coincidence. My mum was in a bit of a hormonal state because of me, and the family had wound her up anyway. Helen's mum was a bit of a wind up merchant too, I think, she kind of taunted them in a way – I don't blame her, by all accounts they were rotten to her – but she gave as good as she got, I think, from what me Nan and me Mum said!

"Helen, doesn't believe that we are all doomed! She thinks it is a bit of a laugh really and says it gives her endless amusement in that place. She's quite a good laugh is Helen …. it will be good to have her out after all this time. Do you know, that if I marry Mon, 'cos she is almost his sister, I will not only be her cousin …. Second cousin? First cousin once removed? Whichever …. but also her sister-in-law! Funny, eh! She says she will write a book and I can do the illustrations!"

What could I say. Did I just admit that I had been a silly old fool for years believing the words of a malicious and ingenious old woman? Did I sacrifice my pride – both professional and personal – in order to put a young woman's mind at rest, and enable her to live her life with a lighter heart? The present seemed, at that moment, to be more important than the past or the future, so what else could I do!

I balked at acknowledging that I had been professionally inept and personally gullible – I was willing to lose a bit of pride, but not throw myself on the funeral pyre as well as on my sword! I said "I think perhaps that it is time to let it go. I can see that perhaps I just wanted to believe it because it would have been a 'first' and an important and momentous phenomenon. The idea was extraordinarily interesting to me, and to my peers. It would have had a profound influence on future work and thinking. …. But I don't believe now that it has been sufficiently well proven – or even proven at all – to make it worthwhile continuing. It seems the right time to say enough is enough, and to stop persevering with an obviously lost cause. I guess in academic speak, the premise has definitely not been proven! I am not sure whether I believed this or not, but it definitely seemed kinder at the time. These young people had suffered enough, and the future had to be left to take care of itself. How I will feel if I read, some years down the line, that more deaths have occurred, I have no idea, but I could not play God – and I would have to leave it in his hands – assuming that He, or She, exists! My experience with Kevin in the church, and Maeve's faith and her assurance that her prayers had been answered had made me waiver, but not, so far, capitulate and venerate!

Epilogue:

I obviously would have been over the moon to be able to give you a definite answer as to the truth or otherwise of the existence of a 'pernicious gene' but unfortunately I cannot. I hope that you will not feel that you have read this story under false pretences, hoping for such a revelation.

Nothing has happened that has made me regret selling my professional soul in order to give Susan some peace, but who can say for the future! That might just mean, however, that I hate to give up on a good thing! Of course part of me hopes that it does not exist, but there is another part – the former academic and professional part that lives in hope …!

I have visited Helen a couple of times over the past few years in Ireland. She is happy there. She shows no sign of wanting to break free and start living her own life – quite the reverse in fact. I think that it suits them all. None more so than Connor.

Connor continues to run the hotel. Siobhan never made a full recovery, and, unfortunately, took her own life, when her baby was just ten months old. They were devastated for a while, but surprise after surprise, Helen and Connor now seem to be forming a very nice partnership (and not only a business partnership!) which delights Maeve. …. Personally I try not to think too much or look too closely at those two facts – the death of Siobhan and the Helen marrying Connor …. Not least because Susan and Helen are soon not just going to be cousins, and 'almost' sisters-in-law' but actual sisters in law too. Both Clement/Colliers together in one family …. Ouch! But, it is the Clarkin Family, and they do seem to lead a fairly charmed and protected life – and perhaps Kevin can keep an eye from somewhere aloft!

Maeve is now, like me, horribly advanced in years. She misses Kevin a lot, and it is not just the years and her inevitable side-lining in the business that has diminished her. He was the spark that ignited her life, and he would have said the same was true of her. They were made for each other. A match made in heaven. If I am in the mood to be really maudlin and pious, I would also add that, despite everything, Helen must have had a Guardian Angel looking out for her too (though he/she must have been on a lunch break when she stabbed Beatrice!) because in hindsight, she was wonderfully lucky ever to have had the Clarkins in her life as well – and to still have them as her saviours, her haven, and her and protectors.

Maeve is less able now to go trekking around the globe visiting her various children and grandchildren, even though, having been 'put out to grass' as she says by Connor, she has all the time in the world. All of her brood seem 'comfortable' - some even well-off - and all are well established and successful in their own lives, families and careers. She now has a total of 22 grandchildren, and so almost every month, one or other of the clan, seems to be visiting her. She has no time to be lonely – except for Kevin.

I'm not quite on my zimmer-frame yet, but certainly the bones are thinning and the joints are creaking. I oil them as much as I can with good wine and good food, and generally don't do too badly for myself. Apparently, though, according to Susan and Mon (who visit now and again with their twin sons, Donovan and Clayton, now aged 4) I should get out more and not have my nose in a book quite so often – too much thinking, apparently, is bad for you. Too much dissection of life, love and destiny makes for a road to unhappiness and despair. I pretend to agree. I did not tell them that I was glad, despite myself, that their twins were boys!

James and Sophia are obviously officially still Helen's parents. She loves them, at a distance, and speaks of them often, but they rarely meet. I think she was disappointed – and surprised perhaps – that James had visited so rarely when she was in 'hospital'. I am not sure of his reason for this – he put it down to the time commitment and/or the fact that it would be upsetting, but in some respects, I think, James reverted back to his previous pre-Elizabeth mentality which pushed into a dark cupboard anything that was not pleasant or beneficial. He always left others – and expected others - to face the more negative aspects of life and smooth out the bumps for him. Sofia carried this burden at home, and Elizabeth before that. The women in his life had always solved his problems for him, and he had got used to that. Anything unpleasant was never to trouble James because he was precious. Sophia had always been a dutiful and diligent step-mother to Helen, but she had never crossed that line which made her a 'mother' no more than Helen had crossed that line that made her a 'daughter'. They are all content, I think, with the current situation: birthday, Christmas, holiday cards, the odd telephone conversation …… not quite strangers, not quite family.

The End.

Made in the USA
Charleston, SC
01 June 2016